The Conspiracy II

Laurence O'Bryan

Copyright © 2020 LP O'Bryan

Ardua Publishing
Argus House, Malpas Street
Dublin 8,
Ireland
http://arduapublishing.com

Ordering Information: Contact the publisher.

This novel is a work of fiction. Any resemblance to actual
persons, living or dead, is entirely coincidental. Real
places and incidents are included only as part of the
fictional story.

Acknowledgements

I'd like to thank my editors Sheryl Lee, Tanja Slijepcevic, Jacqui Corn-Uys, and Alex McGilvery. All remaining errors are mine alone. Special thanks also to my wife, and children, for all their support.

"When evil men advance against me to devour my flesh, when my enemies and my foes attack me, they will stumble and fall,"
Psalm 27:2.

1

West London, May 27ᵗʰ, 2020

Rob McNeil waited. He was in a short line of people outside Emelia's deli on the New King's Road. He and Jackie used to come here regularly to get supplies for breakfast. He found it both comforting and painful to be doing the same thing without her.

The woman behind him nodded as he looked around. "Is this a good place for fish?" she asked, adjusting her blue face mask.

Rob looked into her eyes. There was a smile there. "Yes," he said. "Very good."

"You live around here?" asked the woman. "I just moved in up the road." She was in her late-twenties—a dark-haired beauty, similar to Jackie in a way that made him blink.

"Yeah, I do." His breath caught in his throat.

"I don't mean to be forward," she said. "But I need help with connecting my Wi-Fi." She put her head to one side. She looked forlorn, her blue face mask slightly askew.

"There's an app for that," he said. "Try the Handyman app." He turned away. Something was not right. He hadn't shaved. No woman had ever approached him like that in his life. He didn't turn around again.

On the way back to his house, he walked quickly. He'd seen what might have been people watching him a couple of times in the past few weeks, but no one had made contact with him. All he did was work, eat, and sleep, with memories of Jackie filling his head on endless reels. He'd been told by one trying-to-be-helpful colleague that he was blocking out his grief, but he had to, or it would overwhelm him.

Was that woman just looking for help? Since coming back from Beijing a few weeks before, his life had been drab. Endless working from home, an occasional visit to the lab in Oxford to work on the remaining sample vaccine that had survived the break-in, and only going out to stock up on basics.

The memories of Jackie only made him work harder, usually more than twelve hours a day. But it was good work, and it was saving his soul. And they were getting places, planning phase two trials, in which hundreds of people would be given the vaccine. There was pressure to expand to a phase three quickly after that too. In phase three, the numbers given the trial vaccine would rise to about thirty thousand, but there would be real challenges.

The results of their phase two would change every aspect of any phase three plan. Planning phase three was like walking fast in the dark.

On one visit to the lab a few weeks before, he'd supervised the transfer of a sample of his virus eater into a flask containing a medium of vitamins and sugar so that millions of cells would grow to allow them to create extra vaccine samples. That had been a fraught process. No, every aspect of what he was working on had massive implications. Was that why he was paranoid?

He looked at the surveillance camera high up on a pole at the traffic lights on the corner up ahead. Was the video feed from around his house still being monitored, he wondered? He looked back as he went to cross the road. The woman who'd spoken to him was nowhere to be seen. She'd probably just marked him down as another unfriendly Londoner.

As he neared his house, his phone vibrated. It was a number he didn't know. He didn't answer.

He did that a lot of the time now, to avoid all the sympathetic phone calls from distant relatives and long-lost friends. It wasn't that he wanted to avoid human contact, it was just that he was tired of repeating himself. Tired of the *thank yous* and of endlessly regurgitating upsetting descriptions of what had happened to Jackie.

He'd done enough of it in the first week after he'd got back. He was done with all of it.

When he reached his front door, his phone vibrated again. He looked at it. It was a call from a US number. Maybe he should take it. It could be something to do with his mother in Arizona. He tapped at the phone.

"Holy cow, Rob, do you never answer?" said the voice. It was Jim, the CIA pilot he'd traveled with to China.

"You're lucky I picked up," said Rob.

"I have some news, Rob, my friend."

Rob closed the front door behind him.

"What's up?" he asked.

"No, not yet, how are you, how's your institute?"

"All good, Jim."

"You spend too much time working, so I hear."

They were watching him.

"What do you have for me?"

"You might want to sit down," said Jim.

3

Laurence O'Bryan

Rob put a hand on the wooden banisters. He hadn't turned the light on in the hall, so it was gloomy, with only light from the frosted glass front door coming in.

"I'm sitting," he lied, holding the banisters tight, a dozen speculations jumping through his mind.

"We've seen her," said Jim. "Here in DC."

"Who?"

"Gong Dao. The woman from the Chinese Embassy who visited your wife before she died."

Rob pressed his hand to his chest. His heart had skipped a beat. "I thought she was dead?"

"Apparently not.

"Are you sure?"

"I wouldn't call if you if we weren't." He sounded indignant.

"OK, I'm coming to DC."

"Call me when you get here."

The call cut off. Rob headed up the stairs, fast. His priority for the last few weeks had been getting the vaccine project finished, but he could work on that now from anywhere. They had managers to supervise the vaccine trials.

He had to find Gong Dao, confront her if he could, find out who had ordered her to infect his wife and why. The fact that she'd been listed as dead confirmed they were hiding something. He had to get there before she disappeared again.

It was the least he could do for Jackie.

He looked up flights, and found there weren't many still operating, then paused, and looked out the window. Why had Jim told him about finding Gong Dao? Why did Jim want him back in the United States?

4

2

Dulles International Airport, near Washington DC,
May 28th, 2020

Rob walked quickly through customs and border control. The lines were short and the questions minimal. He had every right to be traveling back to the United States because of his passport. He was waved through. He only had a backpack with him, so he didn't have to wait for baggage.

It was hot and humid when he jumped in the yellow Dulles Express cab. The driver was wearing a black cloth face mask. Rob had bought a pack of blue face masks at Heathrow airport. He adjusted his as he sat into the back, making sure the mask was connected properly at his ears.

"Where to?" asked the driver.

"The Lincoln Hotel on 21st, downtown DC."

He'd called Jim before he left London and had told him when he was arriving. Jim said there would be a room booked in Rob's name at the Lincoln for as many nights as he wanted to stay. He'd also said he'd meet Rob for breakfast at eight the following morning.

The hotel was one of those discreet gray piles that fits in with the discreet gray men and women who ran the city and the nation. Some people call them swamp creatures, probably derived from the nearby Foggy Bottom district, but also because of the great survival instincts of the lobbyists and staffers who would eat each other's hearts for a better job, no matter which party was in office.

His room was all laminated walls and doors, a giant TV he didn't even want to turn on, and dimmed lighting, so you didn't have to see your flaws.

***

There was no room service, because of the virus, and the breakfast buffet bar was closed when he arrived down at the restaurant the following morning. But he had made the right call arriving downstairs with his mask on. People were being waited on at widely separated tables, and only tasking their masks off when their breakfasts arrived and they were eating.

The waiting staff all wore masks too.

He'd arrived early so he could eat a little before the meeting. He ordered just French toast and coffee. He was just finishing it when Jim slipped into the seat opposite. He wasn't wearing a mask. They bumped elbows.

"You don't do masks?" said Rob.

"No, our protocol says we only wear them when we have to," said Jim. "Big crowds, for instance. This place is almost empty." He pointed around him.

"What's the news on Gong Dao?" said Rob.

"You came back quick," said Jim. "But I hate to tell you, she hasn't been seen since she went into the Chinese Embassy yesterday morning."

"Where's the embassy?"

"Straight out of the city, past Cleveland Park; but you won't be going there."

"I could just turn up at the door." Rob put his napkin on his plate and moved his chair under him, as if he would get up and leave.

Jim raised a hand. "No, you don't want to do that." He shook his head.

"Why not?"

"Because I won't give you any more information if you do."

Rob sat back in his seat.

"OK, so why did you lure me back across the Atlantic?"

"There's someone we'd like you to meet." Jim's face was impassive. "Someone you'll want to meet."

"Who's that?"

"You'll find out. Are you ready?"

"You're going to have to tell me a bit more."

Jim leaned forward. "Faith will be there. She'll give you the details. Don't get all paranoid on me."

"OK, let me finish my coffee." Rob took a sip. "Have you seen the protests in Minneapolis? It's all over the internet," he said.

Jim shook his head. "That's a bunch of anarchists trying to tear everything down."

"They do have something to protest about," said Rob.

Jim leaned forward. "There's a lot more to these protests than you think." He looked around. There was no one sitting close to them.

"There's a big Black Lives Matter protest planned for here in Washington tomorrow. We'll be talking about it this morning. Come on, let's go."

He stood and headed for the door.

Rob followed him.

3

Kostromskaya, SW Russia, May 29th, 2020

Vladimir thanked the taxi driver. The man's hand shook as he took the notes that Vladimir passed him. Whether that was because he was an alcoholic or just terrified of Vladimir it was hard to say.

Maybe he'd caught a glimpse of the FSB issued Makarova semi-automatic in a holster under Vladimir's armpit as he got in the cab. Taking a man with a gun to the largest chicken farm in the region might mean someone had made a mistake. The taxi driver would probably tell the story in a bar that evening, or possibly even before that, to his special customers who would listen to him, locals who know people working at the farm.

That would do no harm.

To show people that the Russian state was still interested in what went on at the farm was a good thing. Definitely a good thing.

Stories kept people on their toes. If the population thought there was still a chance of getting a bullet in the back of your head if you didn't do what you were told, it curbed rebellious instincts.

Vladimir headed for the farm manager's building after he exited the cab. Giant sheds made from shiny new sheets of corrugated aluminum extended in rows behind the building, as if to the horizon. Giant silos containing feed,

Vladimir guessed, stood to one side where a truck was being loaded or possibly unloaded. It was hard to tell.

No one stood waiting to greet him at the front of the management building, but he could sense eyes on him. When he looked around, he spotted two men in dirty green rubber coveralls at the end of the silos observing him.

The taxi driver pulled into the car park. Vladimir made a call before going inside.

"When will you be at the farm?" he asked.

"Thirty minutes," came the reply.

He walked across and opened the main door of the management building and went inside. He'd seen a plan of the building so didn't bother to stop at the glass panel reception hole in the wall; he just pushed at the thin door leading to the corridor beyond, turned right and headed for the manager's office.

He counted the doors on his left as he went. When he reached the third door, he jerked the handle and went in.

A shout filled the room. A giant gray-haired man was behind a desk at the far end. A large blonde woman was sitting on his knee with her blouse half open.

Vladimir was wearing a black face mask. The manager and his friend had no masks on.

"Out," shouted Vladimir.

The secretary or administrative assistant, or whoever she was, was still doing up her blouse as she exited the room. Vladimir hadn't shown any identification since he'd arrived, but it was clearly not needed in this situation.

The manager rose, his hands in the air. "I expected you later," he said.

"That's good," said Vladimir. "I like to catch people unawares."

"There's really no need for you to come all the way up from Moscow," said the manager, a foolish smile on his face.

"But this is much more fun," said Vladimir. He pointed his thumb at the door. "Your assistant is from the old school, yes?" He shook his head. "Does anything for her boss?"

The manager grimaced, as if he wasn't sure whether to laugh or cry.

"You have the samples?" asked Vladimir.

"Yes, yes, we have twenty vials, as requested, all contaminated with the new virus that forced us to kill all our stock." He nodded toward the table behind Vladimir. "Look, everything is packed and ready to go."

"How many staff are still here?" asked Vladimir.

"Just the four of us."

Vladimir went to the table, looked at the label on the large Styrofoam box. It was a biological sealing unit with temperature controlling elements inside. Beside it waited a custody sheet, which he signed. It listed the contents as had been requested.

He tested the weight of the box. Yes, it could accompany him back to Moscow on the train. Better that than allowing it out of his sight.

The distant wail of sirens sent the manager to a window. A large, olive green radiation, chemical, and biological incident truck was being escorted into the turning area in front of the building by a wailing police car. Behind them came a prisoner transportation vehicle.

The manager's eyes widened. "This is not a category four incident. I am sure of that," he said, turning to Vladimir.

"You will be detained at a facility not more than a hundred kilometers from your home," said Vladimir in a robotic tone.

The manager shook his head. "Not for six weeks, please. There is work to do here, to restart production. A lot of people depend on their jobs here."

"This facility no longer exists," said Vladimir. "It will be burned, bulldozed over, and declared out of bounds for a period of at least ten years."

The manager's eyes widened. The sound of marching feet echoed down the corridor.

"Don't feel so bad. At least you'll have a friendly assistant with you," said Vladimir.

4

A black Chevrolet suburban waited outside the hotel by the curb, its engine running. Jim looked left and right, then pointed at a rear door for Rob to get in. The vehicle set off quickly once they were inside.

"You don't think there's any real danger here in Washington, do you?" Rob asked Jim, who was peering out the back window.

"We're just cautious by training," said Jim. "You're in my city now. I don't want any mistakes."

"You think the Chinese will want to do me harm?"

"There are over two thousand Chinese agents active in the United States right now. We're watching them all. But to answer your question, no, if they let you leave Beijing it's unlikely they will want to do you harm now."

Jim sat back.

"Where are we heading?" said Rob.

"You'll see," said Jim.

They headed downtown and turned onto K Street. At a six-story glass block, they went down a parking ramp. Their vehicle passed through a metal frame and Jim showed his ID card at a camera. A steel shutter rolled up and they entered an underground parking lot.

"Not many in today," said Rob, looking around. A row of similar vehicles to theirs stood on one side of a mostly empty car park.

"Yeah, working from home is good for a lot of people," said Jim. "We only come in when we're needed." He adjusted his mask and led Rob to an elevator. It required a pass to open. Jim's pass had to be used again for the elevator to move.

He pressed six and a few moments later the elevator doors opened and a wall of air-conditioned air hit them.

"Keep your mask on here, sir," said Jim.

"You guys like it super chilly," said Rob, moving his arms to get his circulation going.

"Yeah, a lot of people want to keep this building cold," said Jim. "It's not the way I'd have it."

He walked ahead, pushed open a door. Beyond was an empty conference room with three large screens at the far end.

They sat. Jim took a keyboard from the long black table and tapped at it until the screens came to life.

There was no audio, just video images of three people, one on each screen. One of them was Faith.

"Before I turn the audio on, I need you to sign something," said Jim. He picked up an iPad from the table, tapped at it.

"Scrawl your signature on this." He handed Rob a white Apple iPad stylus.

On the screen was a box under his name. Rob scrolled up. The language was dense. The clauses numerous.

He speed read it.

After he was finished, he signed. "I see this means you can chop me up into little pieces and bury me in any state I choose," said Rob.

"We can do that, anyway," said Jim. "This just means we can pick the state too." He put a hand up. "No, to be serious, Rob, anything you learn from being in contact with us is considered top secret under the Espionage Act, that is title eighteen of the United States Code."

Rob nodded. "I've signed this before," he said. What he was wondering was what all the enhanced security was about.

"You signed something for the State Department. This is for the agency."

"I thought the FBI looked after internal security matters inside the United States," said Rob.

"I work for a joint task force," said Jim.

"OK, what do you want from me?"

"Hold on." Jim tapped at the keyboard.

Faith gave a thumbs up on the screen. "Good to see you, Rob," she said.

Rob gave her a brief smile. She had done something to her hair. It looked as if a storm had blown through it. It was good to see her.

"Rob, meet Dr. Alan Strong. He runs TOTALVACS, a vaccine manufacturing firm here in the United States. We wanted you two to meet." Jim looked over at Rob and gave him a nod.

"Alan, our friend Rob can give you updates on some vaccine trial plans," said Jim.

"First," said Rob, moving in his chair. This was not going as he'd expected. "Can you give me some background, Dr. Strong. Have you been involved in vaccine manufacture for long?"

Dr. Alan Strong looked at Rob as if he was a homeless man who had been brought in off the street.

"I assumed you'd be up to speed on all this before our meeting," he said. He looked disgruntled as he tapped at something in front of him.

A pie chart replaced his face on the screen.

"You need funding for your phase three trials, Rob," said Dr. Strong. "That's what we can do for you."

"We haven't got a phase three plan yet," said Rob. Not one he wanted to talk about anyway.

"You're doing a phase two for a few hundred participants, Rob. What you need is to move fast to phase three, as soon as early phase two results are in. That will mean planning a full-scale, thirty-thousand participant trial at the same time as running your phase two. This is what we call an accelerated trials program. It's what I think you should be doing."

Rob fought against an urge to tell Mr. Know-It-All what to do with his advice. He looked at the pie chart. It was titled TOTALVACS FUNDING. It had slices for United States government, pharmaceutical industry, charity endowments, and global investment trusts. Each was about the same size and marked with hundreds of billions of dollars.

He had to take this guy seriously.

"You're well funded," said Rob. He paused. Funding was the big issue for doing their phase three right. "So what do you want for funding our phase three?"

"A fifty percent share in an offshoot of your institute created to exploit the breakthroughs you've achieved."

"I don't think so. I have partners, you know," said Rob. He shook his head, his gut tightening at the thought of what a partnership with TOTALVACS might mean—

15

threats and opportunities. "I don't make such decisions alone."

"Work with us and your vaccine will be quicker to market and it'll save a lot of lives," said Dr. Strong. "We all need to work fast, McNeil, put aside our personal differences. Humanity deserves every single shot at beating this virus. Isn't that what you want to do? Save the world. A lot of the vaccine projects currently in the works look like they're going to fail to me. Your one looks promising. Work with us."

Rob didn't answer. The guy had a point. A quicker, funded phase three trial would be a real help.

"You have three days to get their buy-in, Rob. Don't leave Washington," said Jim.

Faith smiled.

"What's your part in all this, Faith?" said Rob.

"I'll be working with you," said Faith. "Putting you two together was my idea."

5

Vladimir put the sample box on the seat beside him. At least this train had proper first-class cabins with lockable doors, wide seats that folded down, and a restaurant, though with limited service. He'd been warned in the station restaurant that he should stock up with a lavash sandwich with cubed lamb and a few bottles of local water before he boarded, as the food service on the train had been restricted to bars of Russian chocolate and hot tea.

He'd taken the advice. Why he'd chosen to go back to Moscow by train was another question. The journey would take almost twenty-two hours.

The reason was paranoia.

The sample he was carrying proved that the Coronavirus had jumped to chickens and could wipe out an entire Russian industry—five-hundred million chickens producing billions of eggs a month and a big fat percentage of the meat for all Russian tables.

Word of his trip and the destruction of the farm would have reached the ears of many interested parties already. He didn't think someone would plant a bomb on a plane in such a short space of time, but a colleague had died in a mysterious plane crash a decade before. It was possible.

And some ruthless people knew Vladimir was heading back to Moscow with samples.

17

Laurence O'Bryan

Better safe than dead.

He put his jacket over the sample box, checked the door was locked, and lay back as the train picked up speed, heading away from the foothills of the Caucuses on the long journey north to Moscow.

6

"You sure know how to put someone on the spot," said Rob. They were being driven back to Rob's hotel.

"You want to sign up, right? It's the patriotic thing," said Jim, hitting Rob's shoulder with his fist.

Rob didn't respond. There were small investors in the institute, but the two big players he'd have to convince, Sean Ryan and Peter Fitzgerald, would take some talking around. Sean was American, but Peter was English.

Dr. Strong was right about one thing though, they needed proper funding for a large-scale phase three trial. Funding applications had been submitted, and they were confident they'd get what they wanted, but nothing was ever sure with medical research until after the funds hit your bank account.

Did Strong know they were waiting for responses?

The car stopped at a traffic light. It was green. Jim peered forward to see what was happening. A stream of people, black and white, many holding placards, were crossing the road in front of them.

"I thought the big demo was tomorrow?" said Jim.

"Getting in some practice," said Rob.

"Some people like to make us look bad," said Jim.

"Who do you mean?" said Rob.

"I'm sure you can guess," said Jim.

"You want to meet for dinner tonight?" said Rob, to get the conversation back to business.

"Where to?"

"There's a Chinese restaurant near their embassy. I want to check it out," said Rob. "The review in the Washington Echo said embassy staff often ate there, so it has to be good, right?"

Jim looked at him, shook his head. "You're not going to go rogue on me, are you?"

"Would I invite you along if I was?"

They moved off from the lights and sped through light traffic toward Rob's hotel. When they reached it, he opened the door, stepped out, and turned to Jim.

"Eight o'clock, the *Eye of the Ocean*. And if Faith's around, ask her to join us."

"What makes you think Faith is in DC?" asked Jim.

"I bet you the tab for the restaurant that she is."

"It's probably closed, anyway," said Jim.

"It is, but still do a great takeaway and we can order their famous spring rolls. We can eat them in one of your vehicles and catch up. Humor me."

Jim was still shaking his head as the door of the black Chevrolet closed and the vehicle moved off.

It was possible they wouldn't show, but they'd probably be intrigued enough to do so. Letting him wander around close to Chinese Embassy staff would make them anxious. Having him under control would be their goal.

He let himself into his hotel room and went straight into the shower. He had a free afternoon and there was a lot he needed to do.

An hour later, after grabbing a ham and cheese bagel from the limited-service coffee shop inside the hotel, he was walking out of town toward the Chinese Embassy. He needed some air. And he needed to think, to come up with a plan.

Two blocks from the hotel, he picked up a cab. It took only fifteen minutes to reach the tree-lined street which held the embassy. The building was an off white, ultramodern design, set back from the road on a street lined with other embassies.

He paid the driver and went to the semi-circular single-story security building, which controlled access to the embassy compound. The gate leading into the compound was closed. A giant red Chinese flag waved from a high flag pole inside the gate. Security cameras pointed in his direction as he knocked at the glass door into the security building. His knock echoed. No one came. He knocked again, louder.

He knew he was acting crazy coming here. Jim and Faith had probably already been notified; they had to be watching this place, but he didn't care. The woman who had probably killed his wife was here, and he didn't believe the Chinese would try to kill him for knocking on their embassy door. But he was sure that if he didn't try to see her, try to get some closure, it would eat at him for as long as he lived.

He knocked again, this time with his fist, sending reverberations through the tall plates of glass that made up the entrance.

A shadowy figure appeared behind the glass. It was a Chinese security guard. He was angry, waving at Rob, motioning him to go away. The guard pointed at a notice taped to the glass to the inside of the door. Rob had read it already. *Because of the Coronavirus, the embassy is closed. Applications for visas and passports can be made online.* A website address was shown.

He knocked again, shaking his head. The security guard shook his head and waved Rob away, more angrily this time.

Rob turned his back on the guard and rapped with his knuckles on the glass.

He continued rapping, taking a break, and rapping at the glass again for five, then ten, then about twenty minutes. Finally, the door to his left opened and a face with a white N95 mask peered out at him.

"You must go away," said an angry voice. "We closed."

Rob rushed to the door and put his foot in the gap. The guard shrieked and kicked at Rob's foot. A steel-capped toe connected with Rob's shin, but he didn't move. The guard raised a weapon, a taser with a yellow snub nose.

"Step back. This Chinese state property. Leave now," the guard shouted.

"I'm not leaving. I must see one of your staff, now. Right now."

A surge of anger poured through him. Behind the guard, two others were rushing toward them. The guard he was struggling with hesitated, as shouts in Chinese echoed from behind him. Rob took his chance and slammed his shoulder into the door. It burst open. He pushed in.

Hands grappled him, threw him face down. He turned as he went down. His shoulder hit the floor first, jarring his teeth.

He'd certainly got their attention.

As he was being searched, he looked out the window and back toward the street. A black Chevy with dark windows was passing slowly by. The noon sun glinted on its chrome. The taste of blood filled his mouth.

7

Rostov on Don, SW Russia, May 29th, 2020

As the train approached Rostov on Don, it grew dark. The gold onion domes of an Orthodox church twinkled on the horizon. The land was flat and green with trees. As they slowed, approaching the station, he could hear people in the corridor outside.

He finished the rest of his sandwich and read the cheap paperback he'd picked up in Moscow before flying down the night before.

He looked out the window as the train stopped with a hiss. The station was mostly empty. A couple of people with red face masks were hurrying toward a side exit. He settled back to finish his sandwich as the train pulled out of the station five minutes later. A spray of twinkling lights flashed by as the city disappeared behind them.

Two hard knocks sounded on the door to his compartment. He covered the sample box with his jacket, made sure his leather holster button was undone, and clicked the door lock open. The door came toward him fast.

"This is a passenger inspection," boomed a voice in thickly accented Russian. "Have your papers ready." The first man who pushed in was a giant with a hard face. It looked as if he could take a few bullets and still pull your head off your shoulders.

"I am FSB," shouted Vladimir, reaching for his wallet and ID. "You are not allowed to disturb me."

The giant put a hand up to grab Vladimir, who stepped back to get out of his reach. The man was clearly used to people stepping away from him as he proceeded to crowd Vladimir toward the window. A second man was now in the compartment.

"We must examine all packages passengers are carrying," said the second man. "There've been a number of lone-wolf terrorist incidents and we have full state authority to check all passengers and cargo traveling from Rostov on Don."

Vladimir put his hand on the giant's chest and pushed. The man swung his hand up to grab Vladimir. He pulled his pistol and pressed it into the man's side.

"Call off your dog or I will blow him apart," said Vladimir with a growl into the giant's face.

The giant either didn't hear him or didn't care. He stepped closer to Vladimir and squeezed him back against the window. Lights flashed behind Vladimir as they passed through a station. The train whistle sounded. An overpowering smell of stale sweat came to him. He licked his lips. His finger twitched on the trigger.

And then, someone grabbed his pistol and bent it awkwardly down.

He pressed the trigger. A deafening burst of gunfire echoed in the compartment.

The giant screamed like a child. He stepped back into the man behind him.

Vladimir looked down. As he'd expected, the two-bullet blast had missed the giant. The blue couch where Vladimir had been lying had two holes in it.

"Sit down, both of you, and put your hands on your head." Vladimir swung the pistol from one man to the other.

They complied. The giant was looking at his jacket. There were two holes in it. He'd been lucky. The bullets had passed closer to him than Vladimir had expected.

The door of the compartment burst open. Two train guards, big men with dark bushy beards, rushed in.

"I'm FSB," said Vladimir. "I am on important state business. Take the handcuffs these men must be carrying and cuff them."

The train guards looked from Vladimir to the two men. One of them started speaking in a local Russian dialect. The smaller of the two men who'd rushed him replied.

The two train guards walked toward Vladimir.

"Identity document," one said.

Vladimir pulled out his FSB ID.

"Apologies, comrade," said the older of the guards.

8

Washington DC, May 29th, 2020

Rob groaned as they pushed him down the white-walled corridor. The embassy reeked of disinfectant. The four men escorting him all had masks on. Masks with respirators. His own mask had fallen off. They didn't seem to care. When they reached the end of the corridor, they opened the door to what looked like an interview room and pushed him in. One of them shouted at him in Chinese and dropped a white face mask on the table.

"I want to see Gong Dao," shouted Rob as the door slammed.

He looked around the room. There were two steel chairs on either side of a bare steel table. Everything was screwed in tight to the floor. A metal box high up in the corner of the room had dark glass sides. The walls were bare and white. He presumed he was being watched. He started pacing around the room. He didn't care what happened to him.

The reality of losing Jackie had been nagging at him more and more with each passing day, undermining him, like woodworm eating into his soul. Until now, he could do nothing about it. Even waking up was getting worse, like waking into a nightmare. No, nightmares were better. They ended.

He had to find out why Jackie had died.

26

Was it his fault?

He kicked at the table leg as he circled, then kicked again at it every time he went around. They'd taken his phone and his thin leather wallet out of his pocket and presumably were breaking into it right now. He didn't care.

He counted the times he kicked at the table leg. When it passed a hundred, his kicks grew stronger. He noticed that it had started vibrating each time he kicked.

At two hundred he could definitely feel the table shifting a little when he kicked it. The side of his foot was hurting now, but he didn't care.

The door to the room burst open. Standing in the doorway was Wang, the Chinese official who'd arrested him in Wuhan.

"What are you doing here?" said Rob.

"I will ask you the same," said Wang. "Please sit now, Dr. McNeil. And stop trying to damage the furniture." He came into the room, closed the door behind him. His mask was red and covered half his face. Rob didn't put his on.

He took a hold of the back of a chair, shook it. "You might have told me why you killed my wife," he said. "Is the concept of truth beyond you?"

Wang sat opposite Rob.

"We didn't kill your wife. Where did you get that crazy idea?"

Rob grunted. "Never mind where I got the idea. It's true. Someone from the Chinese Embassy in London went to my house when I was in Paris, a few days before my wife died, and after that, she came down with a severe strain of Coronavirus and was dead within forty-eight hours."

"First, Dr. McNeil, please put on your mask or I cannot discuss anything with you."

Rob let out an angry groan, but put the mask on the table in front of him on.

Wang continued. "We don't deliberately infect people, Dr. McNeil. I personally reviewed all contacts with you when we met in Beijing. There is no record of anyone from our side going to visit you in London."

"You should look again. The person's name is Gong Dao. She was stationed at your London Embassy last month. My wife told me someone from the embassy came to visit her. You can't deny it." Rob's voice became louder with each word.

Wang made a humming noise. "Wait, I will come back. I will look at the records for our embassy in London." He stood, went for the door.

"You didn't say what you are doing in Washington," said Rob.

Wang turned as his hand gripped the door handle. "I am the liaison officer for our vaccine development program. We have to work together for the future of mankind."

"Nice words," said Rob. "But killing people with impunity is not helping the future of mankind."

The door closed with a bang. It was another one hundred and twenty kicks at the table and circulations around the room before Wang came back.

He didn't sit. "We have no one by the name of Gong Dao working in our embassy in London or working there in any capacity this year. Someone is feeding you a lot of garbage. Was it that Russian troublemaker you were with, or perhaps one of your American friends?"

Rob shook his head. "You're lying. I can see it in your face," he said.

"Dr. McNeil, you are welcome to ask the British authorities to match this person's name with the names of all accredited diplomatic staff in our London Embassy around the time of your wife's death." Wang's tone had hardened. "I understand you are under a lot of stress and suffering from grief at your wife's untimely death. She was very young when she died, but this course of action, trying to make us into a scapegoat, is not a good idea."

Rob looked down at the bare steel table. Wang was reflected on the surface.

Who should he believe—the Russians or the Chinese? Who was lying? His mother had always gone on about telling the truth. His father had too; much good it had done him.

"Well, someone is lying."

"I can prove that your American friends lie," said Wang.

"Go ahead."

Wang smiled. "We know what the Americans want from you," he said.

Rob didn't reply.

"They want access to your vaccine. They probably offered to fund you. But there will be a catch. Yes?" He stopped, examined Rob's face.

Rob's cheek twitched.

"We know what they've been offering other small vaccine developers, Rob. It's always the same thing. They will run the bigger trials. They will use their own phase management teams and you won't even know if the results are accurate or manipulated."

"Why would they do that?"

"They will ask for 50% of the rights to commercialize your vaccine. And there is more they will ask for too." He breathed in deep. Silence descended.

Laurence O'Bryan

Rob could hear a low humming from somewhere in the bowels of the building. "What more?" he asked.

"They will want the right to insert GMOs in your vaccine."

Rob shook his head. "We don't allow genetically modified organisms in our vaccines."

"You will if you accept funding from TOTALVACS. I made you an offer in Beijing to work with us. That offer still stands." He spoke slower now. "And we will not ask for 50%, and we will not insert anything in your vaccine, and you will help supervise the trials. How does that sound?"

Rob put his head to one side. "Will you find out who visited my wife in London?"

"I know that already," said Wang.

"Then tell me," shouted Rob in a burst of frustration.

"When you agree to work with us," said Wang.

Rob stood. "Can I go now?"

"Yes, but don't come back unless you're willing to work with us. No more free help from China for you. We have done more than enough for you already."

He pulled Rob's phone and wallet out of his pocket and placed them on the table.

Rob went to the door, tried the handle. It opened. He walked down the corridor to the security building. He could sense Wang's eyes on him. The guard in the security building opened the glass door as he approached and grimaced as if Rob was some dirt he'd picked up on his shoe.

"Thanks for letting me in, asshole," said Rob, as he passed.

He walked toward the street, pulled off his mask. He looked at his phone. It looked like it hadn't even been broken into.

He could hail a taxi at the next junction or call one.

A squeal of tires echoed as a black Chevy pulled up with blackened windows. A side door opened and a pale, chubby-cheeked face looked out at him. Another man jumped out in front and stood still as if waiting for him to run.

"Please get inside, McNeil. We need to talk to you."

He looked around. "Who are you?" he said.

"Your friend, Jim Stein, asked us to pick you up."

Rob got inside. An agent sat on either side of him as if they were afraid he might try to get out and make a break for it.

"Am I being detained?" he asked.

Neither of the men responded.

"What the hell is this about?" Rob pushed his elbow into one of the men.

"We're taking you to Jim," said the agent he'd pushed.

Ten minutes later they drove into the underground car park of the building on K Street. This time they parked at a deeper level. He was escorted along a corridor that was more like a prison and ordered into a room with no windows and screwed down metal chairs and black camera pods in two corners of the ceiling.

They left him there after giving him a small bottle of water.

He sat on one of the chairs.

His anger was all gone now. He felt drained. He could see what was happening. The reason he came to

31

Washington, to find Gong Dao, was being used to manipulate him. He leaned back. He would see what Jim had got to say and then work out what to do next.

He closed his eyes, tried to meditate. But all that kept coming to his mind were memories of Jackie. He stopped trying. A few minutes later Jim opened the door and came into the room.

"You had us worried," he said. "Are you totally crazy pushing your way into their embassy?"

"If you know so much," said Rob. "You must know the answer to that."

"Look, I get it," said Jim, settling himself into the seat opposite Rob. "You're still deep in grief for your wife. But you're going to be working with us, Rob. You can't be going to the Chinese Embassy. To any embassy. It looked like you were meeting a handler." He leaned forward. "You weren't, were you? Did you meet someone you know inside their embassy?"

"I did. I met Wang, the Ministry of State Security officer who was with us in Beijing."

"*Aaaah*," Jim groaned. "That's not good. What the hell did you talk about?"

"I asked him about Gong Dao, the woman who infected my wife in London. That's why I went there. He said they had no one on their London Embassy staff by that name. And he said they don't deliberately infect people."

Jim whistled, shook his head. "And you reckon he told you the truth, right? I must tell you, it's standard practice that Chinese Ministry of State Security staff are not employed directly at the embassy they visit. They come and go at the order of Beijing, and are not listed with the host country." Jim leaned forward. "Your friend Wang knows this. He's blowing smoke, Rob. What did he offer you?" His eyes narrowed.

"The name of the person who did visit my wife in exchange for me helping with their vaccine research."

Jim laughed. "I have to report all this, Rob. It definitely complicates things. Did you agree to anything?"

Rob rapped the table with his knuckles. "No, I did not, but I have to find out who infected my wife. Why don't you tell me what you know?" He came forward in his chair.

"We don't know who infected Jackie for sure. That's the truth, Rob. We believe a woman, her name was possibly Gong Dao, called to visit your wife soon after you left for Paris. This is the difficult bit." He put his hands on the table as if making a cage with his fingers. "There are a number of factions inside the Chinese Communist Party. This Gong Dao could have been acting for one of those factions."

"I just want to find out who infected her, and why," said Rob. He leaned over the table. "But one thing Wang said got to me, which I'd like an answer to. He said if I work with TOTALVACS, that they'll insist on the right to add genetically modified organisms to any vaccine we create together."

Jim smiled a little. "This stuff is in the contract, Rob." He shook his head. "Don't go and get paranoid on me. So what if they do insert some GMOs? They use a unique GMO biological tracking marker to indicate if anyone who ends up in hospital has been vaccinated with this vaccine or with something else they made. I don't see the problem. It's a good thing. It'll help prove how successful your vaccine is. And they can read the tracking code outside the body, without taking a blood sample. That's progress, isn't it? This is the best deal you're gonna get, Rob. You should sign it."

Rob breathed in, looked at the table. He needed to think. "I should consult my partners. Can I go now? Or am I under arrest?"

"Will you swear you didn't agree to do any work for the Chinese state?"

Rob put his hand up, faced one of the roof cameras. "I swear I didn't agree to do any work for the Chinese state."

"OK, you can go," said Jim. "But no going out tonight. Anyhow, Faith can't make it. I checked. And you have to order by midday to collect dinner from that Chinese restaurant you mentioned. The *Eye of the Ocean*, right?"

"OK, I'll get a taxi back to my hotel."

"We'll drive you. And I'll be at your hotel for breakfast at eight in the morning. And," he made that cage on the table again with his fingers, "I'll have the papers for you to sign with me and with a bit of luck Faith will be with me too."

Rob stood. "I need to go," he said.

Jim escorted him to the underground car park where a black Chevy was waiting with a driver.

Fifteen minutes later Rob was being dropped at his hotel. He had a shower and lay on his bed watching a local news channel. A giant Black Lives Matter demonstration was planned for the next day in Washington DC. Videos showed people who'd already arrived in the city and a small demonstration, going on in front of the White House.

He turned the news off and slipped between the sheets. He needed to sleep. He had plans for the morning.

9

Vladimir saluted the two train guards as he exited his compartment. They'd released the Rostov on Don inspectors as they were only doing their duty, on condition that they got off the train at the next station, which they did, and that they asked no more questions of Vladimir. Vladimir had taken the train guards' names and promised they would be commended for supporting the FSB. He'd also found out the names of the inspectors from Rostov on Don.

It was past midday and warm as he walked through the station. The early Moscow summer had started with long sunny days and people smiling in the streets because of the winter ending. This was the best time to be in Moscow. The promise of summer just ahead, light rains, and a cool refreshing breeze from the river rustling through the linden trees and lilacs that lined the streets.

He would have little time to enjoy the beauty of the city. He had a box of samples to deliver, and then there would be something else. The train station was unusually empty. He knew why. The virus was making people stay home. He had to be part of the solution for this. He had to help things get back to normal.

If word got out that a more virulent strain had infected a chicken farm, there would be even greater fear on

Laurence O'Bryan

the streets. People would not eat chicken and those that did might find they were getting more than they'd bargained for.

It was common practice for inspectors and other visitors, buyers, and feed saleswomen, to go from one chicken factory to the next. For all he knew, all the chicken farms all over the country were infected.

He carried the sample box with two hands and headed to the taxi rank. He gave the address of the virus testing lab which worked with the FSB and arrived there twenty minutes later.

The lab technician who greeted him was in a full hazmat suit. He said little, just took a photo on his phone of Vladimir and the box before getting Vladimir to drop the box into a larger steel container on wheels.

"Call us for the results," said the technician. "Your sample number is 45679."

Vladimir put the number into his phone and asked the waiting taxi driver to take him to FSB headquarters at Lubyanka Square. Hopefully, they would still have some of the Borscht soup that he liked.

On entering the building, however, he was asked to head straight for a meeting room on the sixth floor. He rarely visited the sixth floor. Its corridors were wider, with marble effect floors and the pictures on the walls here were gilded portraits of the previous heads of the various divisions of the FSB and previously the KGB. You only got a picture here if you were dead or had been awarded the Order of Lenin for your services to the state. Most of the people in the pictures were long dead.

One man wasn't, however.

That was Anatoly Chukov, the aging head of the biological and chemical warfare unit of the FSB, and the holder of many state secrets.

Anatoly Chukov was waiting for him in the meeting room. Vladimir had never been in his presence before, but he knew his face from pictures of the podium at the annual ceremonies commemorating the great victory over the Nazi's in the great patriotic war.

"Sit, comrade Vladimir," said Chukov. "I have heard good things about you."

Vladimir nodded. It wasn't exactly a bow, but it was a recognition of the older man's venerable position in the Russian hierarchy. How Chukov had survived Putin's purges was the question he wanted to ask, but he knew he'd be unlikely to get a straight answer.

"You have been having some difficulties recently?" said Chukov.

"Nothing I can't deal with," said Vladimir. Was he aware of what had happened on the train?

"It is imperative." Chukov's voice rose. His jowly cheeks shook as he spoke, as if he had some strange affliction. "That all Mother Russia's children are protected from this evil virus." He pointed at Vladimir. "Thanks to you, we have samples of the new variant, and will be able to send out test kits all over the country in the next few weeks and then burn down any chicken farm this new variant has reached. The men who tried to take the samples from you will be punished and whoever sent them as well. They will wish they'd never been born." His eyes bulged as if they might pop.

"I am pledged to serve my country," said Vladimir with a sniff. "My life belongs to the mother country."

"Excellent," said Chukov. "Because I have another task for you. A task that no one else can do. A task you are most suited for." He leaned toward Vladimir. "But first you will join me in a toast, yes." He reached down beside him and pulled up a brown paper bag. He lifted out a small old-style half bottle of Red Star vodka and two tumblers and, with a flourish of his hand sweeping through the air, he poured vodka into each of the glasses and pushed one across the table to Vladimir.

10

Washington DC, May 30ᵗʰ, 2020

Rob arrived at the hotel restaurant at twenty to eight the following morning. He was half-way through his bacon and eggs when Faith and Jim arrived. He stood, pushed the plate to the side, and put his mask on. Faith and Jim both had black masks on. They didn't shake hands. They greeted Rob and sat.

"Jim has brought me up to speed," said Faith. She put a hand flat on the table. "Thankfully you didn't agree to anything with Wang." She shook her head. "That would have triggered other stuff. TOTALVACS are unwilling to work with anyone who also works for the Chinese."

"What other rules do they have?" said Rob.

"I have emailed you a heads of agreement document, which I hope you will pass on to your partners and get signed in the next few days, Rob," said Faith.

"Anything in it about allowing TOTALVACS to insert GMOs in our vaccine?"

Faith shook her head. "Don't go all wacky on me, Rob. Did Jim not explain this one to you? I don't know if you're familiar with all the new contract terms since this virus started, but the use of GMO trackers is a standard line item now for all contracts for phase three trials. It's not just us."

"Do we get to know what's in the GMOs?" asked Rob.

"Trust is hugely important here, Rob. You have to be willing to trust. I could tell you that you'll know, always, but there could be a supplier switch at the last moment. Things happen. They'll have their reasons. We have to trust that our partners know what they're doing and that it's the right thing."

"Trust and verify, that's the way it works, Faith." Rob pushed his plate further to the side and waved for a waiter to come and collect it.

Faith and Jim ordered coffee.

Rob had his phone out and had opened the PDF Faith had sent him. It had sixty-eight pages. He forwarded it to Sean and Peter, who were both back in London with a short request.

These people want to fund our phase three trial for 50% of the related IP and with this contract. Let's get our lawyers to look it over.

The coffee had been delivered when he was finished.

"We'd like you to come and visit the offices for the joint venture this morning, Rob," said Faith. "We can go there now."

"Aren't there going to be lots of demonstrations in Washington today? The TV says it's going to be crazy."

"The office is two blocks away, Rob. We could walk that far without getting into trouble."

Faith looked into Rob's eyes as if she were looking for something there.

"You should congratulate Faith," said Jim.

"Why?" said Rob.

"She's only got engaged. Her work with politicians has finally paid off. It's a whirlwind romance too."

Faith shook her head. A patch of red bloomed on her cheeks.

"Congratulations," said Rob. "Who's the lucky guy?"

"He works in the Senate."

Jim raised his eyebrows, as if he knew more, but didn't want to say.

"Let's go to the office," said Faith. She glared at Jim, as if pissed he'd said anything about her personal life.

They headed out to a waiting car.

"Will we be reading about your marriage in the media?" asked Rob.

"You bet," said Jim. "That's why I brought it up. You'll be reading about it for sure, and watching it on TV."

"I don't watch that much TV," said Rob. He wondered why Jim had brought up Faith's marriage. Did he think it was a bad idea?

They drove up K Street, where the traffic was light, and pulled up outside the most beautiful modern building Rob had seen in a long time. It had a blue water fountain outside, a mural wall with a giant mosaic of flowers, Van Gogh style, behind the fountain and a smoked glass cladding that shimmered in the morning sun as if it was alive. It looked like something from the future.

"Great building," said Rob.

"Yeah, it is," said Jim. "What until you see inside."

As they walked toward the building, the path around the fountain moved, carrying them forward. The wall with the mural also changed. Now it was a mountain scene, from the Rockies, by the look of it.

Faith peered into a black square in the smoky glass wall when they reached it and a section slid open.

41

"The iris scanner is the best," said Jim, looking at Rob.

Inside waited a wide reception area with steel sculptures and wall paintings with Native American symbols and illustrations. Faith led them to glass elevators at one side of the space and used her iris again to get one to open. She didn't press any button, but the elevator took off.

"It knows where we're going," said Jim.

"I can override it," said Faith. "But it knows where I normally go."

The floor they got out on was the fourth. The reception area here had a big off-white TOTALVACS sign on one wall and two iris scanners on steel poles. There were no humans and no obvious doors.

Faith went to one of the scanners and Jim went to the other. When they finished being scanned, Faith turned to Rob.

"Now your turn. The doors won't open until everyone in our party has been scanned."

"Do they need a blood sample too?"

"Probably," said Jim. "The iris scanner takes our temperature and assesses other health metrics when it scans. Cool, huh."

Rob didn't answer. He expected this sort of intrusion in China, but was surprised to see it in Washington. It probably just meant he'd been immersed in the world of the lab in Oxford for too long.

"Just look at the little red dot," said Faith. "It won't hurt."

Rob walked up to the iris scanner and peered in. The red light blinked. A humming noise sounded from somewhere on the wall and then a low alarm sounded.

"You've broken it," said Jim.

"No, he hasn't. Someone will come," said Faith.

The alarm kept ringing. It was an irritating sound.

Then the noise stopped. A panel in the wall ahead slid open. A tall Chinese woman with blue-tinged hair stepped through and greeted them with a bow. She had on a see-through face mask with green ventilator circles at each cheek.

"Welcome to TOTALVACS," she said. She put her hands out wide in a welcoming gesture. "I came out because we need a blood sample for one of your group before you can proceed to your meeting." She looked at Rob and smiled broadly. "It is only a thumb prick sample, but we need it to ensure any visitors are not asymptomatic carriers of a range of viruses."

Rob put his hand out. He'd given a similar blood sample recently for a test his institute in Oxford was running for a diagnostic tool, so he knew if anyone really wanted his genetic data, all they'd have to do would be to access that data stack.

"You get fast results with this test?" he asked.

"Five minutes for 95% accuracy," said the woman.

"That beats anything we've seen in Europe," said Rob.

"It's still undergoing FDA testing, but our internal testing shows it to be reliable," she said. Then she bowed. "Please wait here while the test runs." She turned on her heel and was gone.

Faith and Jim sat on a white leather bench at the back of the room.

"I passed it," said Jim. "And I had a cough last week."

"Not every virus is Coronavirus," said Faith.

"Wow, that's totally amazing news," said Jim. He stared straight ahead.

"Do you have many Chinese people working here?" said Rob.

"There are quite a few from Taiwan here," said Faith. "Their record in beating the virus is exemplary and they are as committed as hell to helping us beat this thing."

Rob sat down.

"What else goes on here?" he asked, looking from Faith to Jim.

Neither of them replied, they just stared ahead, a fixed expression on their faces.

Rob looked around the room. A white plastic pod in the corner, high up, showed him why they hadn't said any more. Their every action and word were being recorded.

A few minutes later, the sliding doors opened again. The Taiwanese woman came out and waved for them to follow her.

She led the way along a white-walled corridor until they reached a glass external wall, which allowed them to look out over the city. A thin trail of black smoke rose in the air from near the white spike that was the Washington Monument, visible on the horizon.

They walked along inside the glass external wall and entered a large meeting room with a giant screen. A long white table took up the center of the room.

"Your host will be with you shortly," said the woman. She left the room and the door clicked as if locking.

Rob looked around. There were no posters or pictures, just the table and six white chairs with thin white leather cushions.

"How long is this going to take?" said Rob.

"You don't have a lot of patience, do you?" said Faith. She looked at her phone. "Our meeting is due to start in two minutes."

Rob sat, checked his phone, looked at the New York Times website. Reports from the Black Lives Matter protests only a few miles away were saying thousands of peaceful protestors had gathered. They were demanding change.

The door opened and an older black man came into the room. His hair was gray, and he was a little stooped. His suit looked expensive and his glasses were gold-rimmed. The face mask he wore was see-through with green filters like the Taiwanese woman's.

"Welcome to our offices, Dr. McNeil." His accent carried a hint of a southern drawl. "You all following the protests?"

"Yeah," said Rob. "Feels like change is coming."

The man smiled. "Yeah, and my name is Dr. Bishop. I run the TOTALVACS Washington office. I understand the need to protest, especially after so many violent deaths. I was a child who benefited from Dr. King's wave of change, but I also want to make sure our country is defended in this time of crisis."

"No arguments there," said Rob. "What is it you need from me?"

"We have your blood sample, so that's all we need for now. We can clone you in the next few days." He smiled.

Rob shook his head. "You're joking, right?"

Dr. Bishop put his head back and laughed. "You should have seen the look on your face, young man," he said. "Our cloning project is somewhere in the future, but when visitors see our building, they sometimes think we can do anything. We've even been asked if aliens work for us."

He rubbed his hand across the table. "Well, I can assure you we are all too human here. We make mistakes like everyone else."

"Thank you for seeing us, Dr. Bishop," said Faith.

Bishop nodded in her direction, then turned back to Rob. "To answer your original question, I have to be blunt with you. We need you to work with us. I know your partners in England are reviewing our contract, but I also know they are likely to be swayed by your vote. If you are enthusiastic about this partnership, I'm sure you'll be able to get their backing. After all, the virus eater you developed is what we want to test and share."

He was right, of course, Sean and Peter could be swayed if he was convinced, but Rob had his doubts. Was this the time to talk about them? Yeah, it was. They were pushing things very fast, as if they expected him to do whatever they asked without question.

"I've been told you'll have control of the additional ingredients, GMOs specifically, which you'll insert in our vaccine. Is that the case?"

Bishop waved his hand, dismissing Rob's concerns.

"We have been inserting GMOs into vaccines for years. Multiple trials have shown no increase in mortality rates or side effects between the original and the GMO enhanced vaccines. Not all the new inserts are tested, but we believe the benefits, tracking in particular, far outweigh any dangers."

"GMO vaccines have been linked in some studies to the appearance of more virulent strains of the target virus," said Rob.

"We are aware of the dangers, but the potential for such mutations exists in non-GMO vaccines as well," said Dr. Bishop.

"It's a matter of trust, Rob," said Faith.

"Sure, but we'll need data on anything you add—chemical formulas, suppliers, test results, everything," said Rob.

"Sure, you'll get it all. We do everything the right way, Dr. McNeil," said Bishop. "Your fellow citizens of the United States need you to bat for them. And not just for our country, for the world too. Let's do this."

Rob could feel the pressure building, like a coffee pot coming to the boil. They were all staring at him, their mouths half open, willing him to agree on the spot.

"An initial payment of ten million dollars, to become an expert consultant for this project, will be made to your bank account on the agreement proceeding," said Bishop.

11

Vladimir left FSB headquarters at a little after nine that night. An FSB plane would take him overnight to Washington Dulles airport. He would be accompanied by a new liaison officer for the Russian Embassy in Washington. The woman was tall, black-haired, and stern looking, as you'd expect from a first-class graduate of the Moscow Institute of Physics & Technology with a double PhD and a two year diplomatic service training program under her belt.

He'd been told about her after leaving Comrade Chukov. She would be on the plane to Washington with him. He was designated as her driver. That was his cover. She would probably be happy with this, as she'd never had a driver before.

Vladimir would not spoil her enjoyment of this. The less she knew, the better.

He passed by his apartment on his way to the airport, visited with his friend opposite to make sure she was still alive, but kept his mask on the whole time and didn't go further than her hallway. He found out that the night visits to his apartment by colleagues in the FSB had stopped. No one slipped in when he was out anymore.

"I am the one getting the most men coming to see me again," she said.

"Stop seeing clients until I get back," he said. "There is a new variant of the Coronavirus spreading here in Russia. It will be in Moscow in days. If you want to die, keep seeing people." He pulled a wad of dollars he'd been given and peeled off five one hundred dollar notes.

"You never paid me before," she said, a smile on her face. It was the first smile he'd seen her giving him in months.

He pulled the notes back as she went to grab them. "Do you agree not to see any men when I'm away?"

She nodded, eagerly. "I didn't know you cared," she said, laughing.

"Don't get your hopes up," he said. "I just don't want to come back and find everyone in the building dead because of you." He gave her the money.

"I have a very good chess partner on the third floor. I want him to be alive next winter, understood?"

She nodded, pushed the notes into her bra, and gave him a wonky smile.

After showering, changing his clothes, collecting his backpack, and checking his windows were all closed and electrical items unplugged, he headed down to the waiting FSB car. His friend waved at him from a high window as he looked up, before he climbed into the vehicle. It was almost as if she liked him. He let out a derogatory grunt. She probably treated all her big-spending clients that way.

On the flight he got to know Olga, the new liaison officer. She was chattier than he expected, probably because of the excitement of being whisked to the United States on a Russian State plane.

She'd probably expected something simpler and smiled proudly to herself for much of the flight. He listened to her tales of scaling the heights in the Russian diplomatic

49

corps training center. She didn't ask him any questions about his background. With his new tight military haircut and older, craggy face, she would assume, correctly, that he was ex-military and incorrectly that he'd been given this plum driving role by a high up relative or comrade from his days on the front line.

He didn't tell her that he wouldn't be driving her around Washington at all or that he was the reason they were traveling by government jet. He would let her figure it out later. And this way, if she was asked at Dulles Airport what their relationship was, she could reply honestly, with that fresh-faced look only a truthful person has.

12

Rob put his hand up. "OK, I am willing to do everything I can for my fellow Americans," he said. "But don't expect us to fall for anything your lawyers come up with. I will fight to make sure my institute gets a fair deal, and when the deal does go through, which I will push for, you can pay that ten million dollars to the True American fund for third world vaccine deployment." He paused. "And I want one other thing."

"What's that?" said Bishop.

"That I be involved in the phase three trial's management and receive the trial reports."

"Sure, this we can do. But I also have a request of you," said Bishop.

The room went quiet.

"What is it?" said Rob.

Both Jim and Faith wore amused expressions as if they were taken aback by Rob's donation of his ten million dollar payment.

"We want you to go back to your friend in the Chinese Embassy and agree to work for them. Offer to share whatever information you extract from us in exchange for being part of their vaccine development program."

"Are you serious?" said Rob. "You want me to tell them about our agreement?"

51

"Yes, they suspect already that you've been recruited. So they know about us. This will make you more valuable to them. They prize high-level connections."

Rob let out a low whistle. "Who else will know about this? If I'm questioned for talking to the Chinese, will you back me up?"

"Yes, we will. Refer any requests for confirmation of your status to Jim or Faith. Both the CIA and FBI are on board with this."

Rob looked at Faith and Jim. They nodded in agreement.

"I can't just turn up at the Chinese Embassy again," said Rob. "Is that what you want me to do?"

"No, we don't expect you to try to break in again. We've moved your belongings from the hotel to the Wilshire Creek Condos complex not far from their embassy. It's owned by a Chinese billionaire and is where visitors to their embassy from Beijing usually stay. They have a reception you can leave a message for your friend at. That will get it to him, I am sure of it."

Rob looked around. "Is all this conversation being recorded?"

"Yes," said Bishop.

"I want it clear that I am doing this at your request," said Rob, looking up at one of the camera pods in a corner of the ceiling.

"You can ask them for information about your wife," said Faith. "We want you to find out everything you can about what happened to Jackie."

Rob didn't respond for a minute. He was thinking about the implications of what he'd just agreed to.

"I am not going to give them details of our trials."

Jim put his hand up to intervene. "We want you to discuss only your work up to today. Say nothing about any ongoing work with TOTALVACS. It is likely, given the break-in at your institute—and don't start me on the subject of your security—it is likely that they know the exact makeup of your vaccine. That is also what you spoke about in Beijing and Moscow." Jim paused, then continued at a slower pace. "Just repeat what you told them there, what you know they already know."

"You think they'll fall for that?" said Rob.

"You'd be surprised," said Bishop. "I had someone who worked for me a few years ago who became part of their thousand talents program to recruit high-flyers. In the end, all he had to do was give the same lectures he was giving at MIT, but in Beijing."

Rob didn't like it, but anything that might help him find out what had happened to Jackie had to be considered. And if he missed this opportunity, it might never come again.

"OK, I agree, and on the terms discussed." He pointed at the camera pod. "Can I have a copy of this recording?"

"Sure," said Jim. "I'll have it emailed to you."

Dr. Bishop stood. "You are now officially part of our family. You may use this office as you need it. You'll have 24-hour access with supercomputer power available and concierge services to arrange travel and transport." He nodded at Rob. "You made the right call for this country. Millions of lives depend on us having a bridge to the Chinese vaccine effort. You are totally ideal for this role. They would not accept anyone without your type of credentials. Thank you for your service, Dr. McNeil."

He escorted them out. They exited the building and climbed into a black Chevy with darkened windows that pulled up just as they reached the curb.

Twenty minutes later they were pulling up at the Wilshire Creek Condos.

13

The flight from Moscow Vnukovo airport was uneventful, but long. They stopped at Shannon in Ireland for refueling. The Russian Ministry of Foreign Affairs' Cessna Citation, donated by an oligarch, had a seating capacity of eight. A party of four replacement embassy staffers were the only other passengers.

Vladimir was happy not to have to wait for a connection at Paris or elsewhere, with the chance of getting quarantined if they took a layover in the wrong city.

He went through the United States passport check last. If there were problems, he didn't want the others held up. But there weren't any. The passport checker put his new diplomatic passport through a scanner, and he went through without even having to stop at customs. The required declarations had already been made on behalf of all the embassy officials, stating that they weren't carrying dutiable items.

The embassy had also arranged for a shuttle bus to take them to the staff residence. The light blue bus was waiting outside the main terminal arrivals area. The new liaison officer was deep in conversation with one of the other embassy staffers, so Vladimir went to the back and looked out the back window. As expected, an FBI vehicle was right behind them. It was one of their new Chevys with video capture cameras near the front fender. They may have seen a warning flag about him already and might even know about his visit to China and to the United Kingdom.

His cover of being a driver would really only be useful for non-state actors in the United States and for internal purposes within the embassy.

The Russian Embassy in Washington is located in Westchester, north east of the city center, on leafy Wisconsin Avenue. The embassy is a pale-gray, eight-story modern block set back from the street. The yellow apartment blocks, farther up the slight hill, housed some of the low-level embassy staffers.

Vladimir had been allocated a single person's apartment in one of those blocks. He exited the shuttle bus with the other staffers at the entrance to the apartments. It was late afternoon. He'd been traveling for twenty hours.

As he followed the group of chattering embassy staffers to the apartment block, an FBI vehicle pulled up with a squeal of brakes near him. A smoked glass passenger window rolled down and a voice called his name.

"Vladimir, over here."

He looked around. The staffers hadn't noticed, yet.

He stood a few feet from the vehicle, bent down, and looked in. A bull-necked agent stared back at him.

"No funny business while you are here, Vlad. We know the type of work you do."

"I'm just a humble driver," said Vladimir. "Do I not get a warm welcome to your great democracy?"

"Save it for someone else, Vlad," said bull-neck as the window closed.

Vladimir looked around. Things were very different here from the precautions everyone was taking in Moscow. Few people on the street were wearing masks and the FBI men hadn't been wearing them either. He'd seen some people at Dulles Airport wearing them, but not many. He took a deep breath. One good thing you could say about America was that you could do whatever you wanted, as long as you were prepared to face the consequences—including death.

The liaison officer was holding the door for him into the apartments. He hurried in and thanked her.

"Is that your only baggage?" she asked.

He patted his bulky backpack. "All I need is here. I don't expect I will have the big social life you will."

"I don't expect any social life, apart from appearing on VK," she replied. "Is it allowed in the United States?"

"They don't block our social media sites," said Vladimir. "You can show off about your new job all day there."

"I'll see you when I need a driver." She shook her head. "But I don't expect we'll be going out much with the virus." She was looking at him and blinking, as if finally wondering why a driver had been allocated to be with her in the middle of a pandemic.

Vladimir's rooms were at the back of the building, on the third floor, with a large window facing the embassy compound, so he couldn't be easily observed by the various agencies and other nations who watched Russian Embassy staffers.

He'd once heard someone say that there were at least ten countries spying on their Washington Embassy at any one time, from rival petroleum states to the big powers. He would have to careful here. After a shower, he checked the time was right, then picked up the encrypted cell phone waiting for him and dialed 112 for embassy security.

"I'm ready," he said.

Laurence O'Bryan

"Good," the voice at the other end replied in Russian.

Before he exited the room, he looked at himself in the mirror. His new wig was a mop of unruly hair tied back in a ponytail. His brown, ill-fitting janitor's overalls had All Services on the sleeves and across the front. He headed down the service stairs to the basement. The door out to the underground car park was open. The All Services vehicle was waiting. They'd sent a man into the building with a ponytail twenty minutes before. Now Vladimir would be leaving instead. The man who'd been dropped off would go out the front door, without the overalls. You can get a lot done if you pay the right price.

He got in the back of the service vehicle and said nothing to the driver. He was dropped off near Farragut Square, at the K Street intersection.

14

Rob's room was bigger than he expected. It was on the second floor at the end of a long corridor. He had seen no one since arriving. The entry card he'd been given by Faith had opened the apartment reception area, which was empty of people when he passed through, and had allowed him entry to his room.

The room had a high double bed, a table, desk, two chairs, a TV, and plastic notices pinned to the wall near the door. A small balcony overlooked a line of black pine trees at the back of the condos.

He noted his clothes and washbag were all in the room and examined the wall notices. They were in Chinese characters and English. One section, at the end of the last notice, gave information on how to contact another person staying in the complex. Following the instructions, he went to the landline, pressed zero, and left a voicemail for the reception asking for it to be passed to a Wang Hu, if he was staying in one of the condos.

Contact me, was the message he left.

He showered, then went for a walk in the nearby Rock Creek Park. It was busy with afternoon walkers. He found a coffee shop on the way back and enjoyed a double espresso and a bar of Hershey's to keep his sugar levels up.

When he got back to his room, the message light was flashing on the phone.

As he was about to pick it up, a knock sounded on the door. He looked out the spy hole and saw someone bending down in front of his door. He stepped back and watched a slip of yellow paper come through under the door. *The Pool—Now,* was all it said.

He found a map of the complex and located the pool in the gym area at the rear. He closed the door to his room and made his way there, wondering who had summoned him. The pool wasn't easy to find. There were few signs and lots of branching corridors. Everyone he met was wearing a face mask here, and they didn't seem happy to be stopped, even if he was wearing a mask and stood well back when he asked for directions.

Both of the people he asked were Chinese. Both told him, with a glum shake of their heads, that the gym and pool were closed. He said he just wanted to see them.

When he finally found it, the door to the gym was open and the door inside, leading to the pool observation area, where parents could watch their youngsters swimming, was also open. The pool had a blue plastic cover over it. There was a strong smell of chlorine in the air.

The observation area was a tiered set of seats stretching along one full side of the pool. Wang was standing about half-way along the middle tier of seats.

When Rob arrived near him, Wang turned to him. "I didn't expect to see you again, Dr. McNeil. People tend to stay away from me after I've tried to get information out of them."

Rob shrugged and peered at Wang, who was clearly wearing makeup, as the marks on his face were not visible. His mask was black with a red star at the mouth.

"You didn't carry out your threats, so I figured you were more bark than bite," said Rob. "And you made me an offer I'd like to talk to you about."

Wang shook his head. "Your friend caused over a million dollars' worth of damage to Wuhan airport when his plane exploded. Who will pay for that?"

"I don't know anything about it," said Rob. "But I do know I can help you."

Wang looked uneasy. "You'll have to prove yourself," he said. "How do I know you have not been sent to me?"

"I'll prove it." He pulled out his smartphone. He went to his photos and showed the pic of the TOTALVACS building he'd taken earlier.

Wang peered at it. "What are you doing with them?"

"I'm working for them as a consultant too."

"We know these people. They are putting a lot of money into their vaccine candidates. What do you need us for?" Wang's expression hardened.

"I'm determined to bring justice to whoever killed my wife," said Rob.

"You won't let it go, will you?"

"I just want to understand what happened; why she had to die," said Rob.

"So you can stop blaming yourself?" said Wang.

"I don't blame myself," said Rob, angrily. He stepped nearer to Wang. "But if I find out someone from China was behind my wife's death, I will track them down and find a way to make them suffer like she did." The frustration and anger were still there. Every time he thought about the possibility that someone had infected her deliberately, he wanted to break something.

"I will find a way."

Wang shook his head. "I am sure you will, Dr. McNeil."

They stared at each other. "But I can tell you this. You will not be coming after me, because I was not involved in your wife's death."

"I was told a woman named Gong Dao, from the Chinese Embassy in London, gave my wife the virus." Rob's fist was up. It was shaking.

"Do you believe everything the Russians tell you?" said Wang. His eyes were wide with mock surprise. "A Chinese woman named Gong Dao may well have visited your wife. She may even have infected her, but this was not an official Chinese government plan." He looked around.

"Think on this, Dr. McNeil. Many other people, not members of the Chinese Communist party, may be seeking to delay or stop your vaccine production in America."

"Why?"

"There are billions at stake. Many people will want other competing vaccines to fail."

"Like the Chinese Communist party perhaps?"

Wang shook his head. "We don't need to stop your vaccine to prove we are superior. The world knows already we have the best system for dealing with the challenges of this century, including the virus and many other things you struggle with."

"You are deluded," said Rob.

"Our form of government is superior, Dr. McNeil. It is obvious to all. You may have the freedom to do what you want here in America but many more of you will die for this freedom. We control every life and we will live because of that. I know which I prefer."

"A living death," said Rob. "Without freedom we are robots."

Wang shook his head.

"So how do I find out who gave Gong Dao her orders?" asked Rob.

Wang waited a few seconds before replying. "What do you Americans say; you scratch my back and I will scratch yours? Is that right?" Wang gave him a thin smile.

"What do you want?"

"There is something you can take for me into the TOTALVACS offices here in Washington and put it somewhere where people talk." Wang pulled a black, palm-sized clock out of his pocket. It was a simple design, the type of clock you would see in many offices on a desk or in a kitchen.

"Put it where? What will it do?"

"It listens and it relays Wi-Fi passwords tapped into phones."

"You want me to plant a spying device?"

"No, not that. This is a better idea," said Wang. "You bring it to whoever you work for at TOTALVACS and you tell them I gave it to you and what I asked you to do. This way they will trust you."

"What is it you want me to do?"

"As you can see, nothing, except what I asked, for now. Tell them you fooled me and then keep me in the loop about your vaccine progress."

"That's it?" Rob didn't feel convinced.

"We need to build bridges too," said Wang. "Let us say we will drive things over it later."

"So, what can you tell me about the people responsible for Jackie's death? How do I find them?"

"You know how to already, Dr. McNeil." Wang looked pleased with himself. "Simply think about who sent you to Paris."

15

Vladimir headed south, circling Farragut Square, looking for any sign of the looters reportedly defacing stores and vehicles. The latest report stated that a group of about twenty-five had broken from a Black Lives Matter protest and were heading toward Farragut Square, perhaps in the mistaken belief that the statue in the square of General Farragut was a Confederate General, not a Union Admiral.

Whatever the reason, the looters had spray painted some vehicles and the windows of some stores on the way here. As Vladimir walked along by the side of the square, he spotted some homeless people with unkempt hair sitting on two of the seats on one of the paths through the square. He pulled up the hood on his sweatshirt and pulled a hundred dollar note from the roll in his pocket.

Two Washington DC police officers were standing beyond the group of homeless. If he was stopped by them or anyone else, he could truthfully say he was looking for information about the rioting for his embassy. The truth is the lie.

Two of the homeless men looked at him with suspicious eyes as he approached.

"Where are the protestors?" he asked.

Someone cackled an indistinct reply. Another man with greasy jeans slouched toward him, eyes wide, pupils dilated.

"I got a Benjamin for anyone can tell me which way they went."

"That's easy, man," said the sloucher. His face was thin and dirty. He pointed toward 17th Street.

Vladimir held the $100 note out.

"Anyone else know anything better?" he asked.

"Yeah, that doper's a born liar," said a young woman with stringy black hair and a baggy t-shirt dress. "They headed down Connecticut Avenue five minutes ago."

Vladimir dropped the $100 note on the ground and stepped back. He walked away as a scuffle broke out. He headed down Connecticut Avenue.

Ten minutes later he spotted a small crowd of young people at a Starbucks and stood to the edge of the crowd with his hood up, looking for a leader. There was an argument going on. Some of the young people were looking at their phones, presumably trying to figure out where the real Black Lives Matter action was. A tall, young white man with a hipster beard, was poking at an overweight, bushy-haired black man wearing a BLM t-shirt.

"We gotta get that statue down," he was saying.

"We gotta go back to the Mall," said the black man.

Vladimir walked up to them. He leaned toward the black man, one hand out in front of him, palm up, appealing to him. "I got an idea, way better than this Union Admiral your friend wants to take down."

He made a fist. His accent was foreign, but he spoke clear English. "I'm talking about doing something to the people who deliberately killed many, many brothers."

The young man was listening intently now. "What do you mean?" he said.

"There's something worth defacing just two blocks from here, and I'll give you a nice fat contribution to thank you for standing up for minorities. I know you need help." He raised his fist again in solidarity.

The white boy looked him up and down. "You some pig instigator, trying to get us all arrested or something?"

Vladimir pulled up his sweatshirt at the side. A wide scar ran around his lower stomach area.

"No way, man," he said. "I was poisoned by big pharma and my woman died. I just want to see their fancy offices get some graffiti." He put his hands up. "No serious stuff. Nothing really bad. Put BLM and curses all over their fancy glass, that's all."

"It'll be the easiest money you make all year." He waved them to come closer. "Get your friends to throw a few firecrackers outside the place too."

The two young men looked at each other.

"What do we get?" said the white boy, his eyes narrowing.

Vladimir pulled a small roll of notes out of his pocket. He showed it for a second, then wrapped his hand around it. "Don't try to take it from me, guys. I was in special forces and I can poke your eyeballs out before you can scream for your mommies."

He put the roll of notes away. In the distance, three police officers on bicycles were heading their way.

"Are you in?" he asked. "Just turn left onto K Street and look for the building set back from the street with a blue water fountain outside."

16

Rob had a conference call with Peter Fitzgerald and Sean Ryan, his partners at the institute, coming up at three that afternoon, eight p.m. London time. It was a Sunday. Rob had requested an emergency meeting to discuss the offer from TOTALVACS.

He also wanted an opportunity to confront Peter, who had sent him the invitation to go to Paris.

The invitation had been genuine, but it was likely, given what Wang had said, that someone on the French side had asked to make sure it was him that ended up getting it. He needed to understand what Peter knew about it.

As he waited for the online video meeting to start, his mind wandered to the first time he'd met Peter Fitzgerald, just before he'd been recruited to join the institute. It was supposed to be a friendly lunch, as Sean Ryan had already interviewed Rob twice. Rob remembered it all clearly for various reasons, including where the meeting had taken place, in a high-class Chinese restaurant near Harrods in London.

Peter had known the manager. He'd also argued with Rob.

He even remembered the argument. It was to do with the ethics of gain-of-function research, the process of making a mild virus into something much worse, to study it.

The United States National Institutes of Health had, a little while before that, allowed gain-of-function research to be restarted.

Rob was against the whole idea of adding extra, potentially highly lethal functions artificially to viruses.

Peter had been all for it. It had become a recurring theme between them. But at the back of his mind, Rob had often wondered if Peter disagreed with him, because he wanted to make the decisions.

Rob's smartphone buzzed on the table in his room. It was an alert for the start of the Zoom meeting with Peter and Sean. He spent the first ten minutes bringing them up to speed on what had been happening.

"The offer from TOTALVACS is predatory," said Peter, in a dismissive tone. "I am one hundred percent sure we can get United Kingdom funding for phase three research."

There was silence from Sean.

"I definitely say no to the offer," said Peter. "Let's stay independent. Conversation over."

"No, it's not. And anyway, if we do get funding in the UK," said Rob, a clear hint of anger in his voice, "we'll have to give away similar control. The contracts with the big pharma companies are all the same. What do you think, Sean? Do you want to get into bed with one of Uncle Sam's friends or Boris'?"

"Perhaps we should keep it in the UK," said Sean.

Peter snorted, happily.

Rob breathed in deeply, controlling his frustration. Turning this into a shouting match would not help. But what could he say to turn things around?

"I developed this. I think I should get some say into what happens to it," he said. "And yes, I think we do it. It gets us a fast manufacturing deal, which is what we need, and we get to see it in the field faster. On balance, it's the right deal."

There was silence.

Then Sean spoke. "It's your call, Rob. You did develop it. I'll back whatever you decide."

"Are you sure about that?" said Peter. "This is a big decision."

"I have to support Rob," said Sean. "That's the end of it."

Rob clenched his fist. He'd won.

Peter's mouth was opening and closing like a fish.

"Before you go, Peter," said Rob. "Did you know these people in Paris who invited me to speak there just before Jackie died?"

"What, what?" said Peter. "You mean last month, yes?"

"Yes, Peter."

"Well, well, if I remember right, it was a Chinese vaccine scientist working in Paris who recommended you for that. It was a prestigious engagement. Should I not have passed it on?" He sounded bitter.

"Do you remember the name of the person who asked for me?" said Rob.

"No, why should I? I don't remember all the details of emails from a month ago." He sounded flustered now.

"Can you forward me the request?" asked Rob.

"Yes, absolutely, old boy, but . . ." There was a hesitation.

"Now that I think about it, the connection came in via WeChat." Peter's voice trailed off.

"I didn't know you were on WeChat," said Sean.

"Yes, my partner encouraged me to get on it."

69

Rob rubbed his chin. Of course, Peter's new partner was a Chinese doctoral student at the University of London. Peter had met him at the Confucius Institute, where he'd been learning Mandarin.

"Send me the person's name who suggested me for the meeting, will you?" said Rob. "I want to thank him."

"I'll get it to you when I can," said Peter, sounding annoyed again. "Is that all?"

"Yes," said Rob.

"Please send us the contract for electronic signature," said Sean. "You'll get it back at the end of the week."

"Get the lawyers to go over it quickly," said Rob.

"I will. And we'll make sure they aren't trying to slip something in the contract they didn't tell you about."

"Great," said Rob. He closed the call.

17

Vladimir walked with his new friend to K Street and showed him the building.

"I have to go," he said. "But promise me you won't do any more than graffiti the building and let off a few firecrackers."

"Sure," said the young black man. "I'm the artist here. Street art is what I do. What would you like us to write on their perfect glass?"

"Vaccines kill too," he said. "Stuff like that."

"You crazy man," said the black guy. "Vaccines save millions of lives."

"He's paying. We play the tune," said the white guy.

Vladimir held the roll of hundreds out. "Show me your paints," he said.

The black man pulled his shoulder bag around and opened it. It was full of spray cans with paint all over them. Vladimir handed over the money.

"I'll be watching," he said.

"Yeah, cool, man," the black man said, sharing the notes with his white friend. "We gonna head up there anyhow."

Vladimir watched them turn onto K Street.

71

Laurence O'Bryan

A glow of warmth ran through him. They really had no idea what they would be part of. It was easy manipulating people with a grievance.

The All Services vehicle was waiting in the next side street. He got in the back and the vehicle moved off. At the next lights, it turned right. At the intersection, it turned left and pulled up opposite the TOTALVACS building. The members of the BLM crowd were singing, dancing, and approaching TOTALVACS. The area outside the building was otherwise dead, but as Vladimir watched, some of the movable cameras on the top of the building angled down for a closer look at the approaching crowd.

The security team inside would have plans ready in case the building was attacked, but they didn't have a plan for a graffiti attack. And that was what happened. The whole BLM crew swarmed around the fountain and the mural. Black Lives Matter was soon scrawled all over the fountain, the mural, and the glass sheet wall of the building in a rainbow of colors.

Across the street, a technician in overalls had emerged from the All Services vehicle. He propped a ladder against the traffic lights at the intersection. He climbed up it and cleaned the lights with a cloth, then took a small black box, the same color as the traffic light pole, and fitted it above the traffic light, facing both the front entrance and the underground parking lot entrance to the TOTALVACS building.

The technician and the vehicle were gone a few minutes later. Even passersby paid them no attention. All eyes were on the protestors defacing the office block opposite.

Vladimir sat in the back of the vehicle on a stool bolted to the floor and looking at a screen on one wall as it rode slowly down K Street. The screen flickered again and again. Then the image turned crystal clear, showing the protestors outside TOTALVACS. As he watched, a black SUV Town Car exited the car park of the building. The screen automatically focused, and when the vehicle turned, a second smaller screen opened, with a view from one of the side cameras.

A box popped up on the screen. It was a request for an access password.

"What's the password?" Vladimir shouted at the technician who was driving them back to the embassy.

"Wait," came the reply.

A password manager filled the password box automatically. He pressed return.

The license plate of the vehicle popped into a box on the left of the screen.

The system was now patched into the DC District Department of Transportation traffic management system. It could track any vehicle across DC's eleven-hundred miles of roadways. Live traffic reports were a key part of the camera network's public-facing benefits. Tracking target vehicles was a less commonly known benefit.

"You don't have to watch it," said the man in the front of the vehicle, without turning to Vladimir. "The plate numbers and travel destinations of all vehicles entering and leaving the TOTALVACS building will be available for download from the cloud as you need them."

"We paid enough," said Vladimir. "It better work."

18

Rob woke early the following morning. He made coffee in his room, then called Faith and asked for a car to pick him up.

It arrived ten minutes later.

At the TOTALVACS building, a team of cleaners was working on the outside of the building. Faith was waiting for him inside.

"Did you see the graffiti?" asked Faith, as she walked him to the onsite restaurant. Part of it was closed—the fresh hot food section—but there were plenty of coffee choices, individually wrapped fruit, pastries, and Subway style sandwiches.

"How could I miss it? Very colorful," said Rob. "The anti-vaxers must be happy. Counting the downsides of vaccines has always been more interesting the counting the millions saved."

"We're lucky that's all the damage they did." She leaned toward him. "We reckon an instigator told them to come here."

"Isn't that what every building owner thinks?" said Rob.

"Did anything happen at your apartment?"

"I just met with Wang."

"Go on."

He told her about his conversation with Wang and that Wang had wanted him to plant a clock in the TOTALVACS building. He took the clock from his jacket pocket and gave it to her.

"I also found out I was deliberately recruited to go to Paris, most likely so someone could infect my wife with the virus." His voice trembled with anger as he said the words.

"You don't know that for sure. Why would someone want to infect your wife?" Faith sat on a low leather sofa, one of a set of two, facing a coffee table. A row of similar seating options ran along the wall of the restaurant.

"Maybe they didn't think she'd die so quickly. Maybe they thought I'd catch it from her when I got home."

"They wanted you infected?" Faith looked unconvinced.

"Someone else wanted my vaccine research project to fail. That's my best guess. So they push me off the road. It fits."

"You think it's the Chinese?"

Rob shrugged. His phone buzzed. He thought it might be Sean in London with some news on the contract. It wasn't.

Some strange number had sent him a text message: STOP THE PROJECT OR YOU WILL SUFFER AS YOUR WIFE DID. FRIENDLY WARNING.

"Christ," said Rob. "This is too much." Anger boiled inside him.

"Look at this." He turned his phone to Faith.

She leaned forward and examined the message.

"Have you had others like this?" she asked.

"No."

"Forward it to me, and any others like it you get."

Rob forwarded the message. Faith tapped at her screen when it arrived. "I've sent it for tracing. We'll find out where it came from, if not who sent it," she said.

"I reckon that's the bastards who killed my wife," said Rob, spitting out each word. "Tell me anything you find out about them."

"Let's go and see Bishop. He's waiting for an update," said Faith.

They dropped their paper coffee mugs in the recycling chute and headed up a slow-moving walkway to the next floor, which had open-plan offices.

"You'll be able to use any of the desks along the wall," said Faith. "The first time you turn on a screen, your iris will be scanned and access rights to the TOTALVACS cloud provided." She pointed at a set of glass doors to one side of the shared desks. "Bishop and the other managers have their offices there."

Rob heard a noise and turned.

"Getting the tour?" said Bishop approaching, bouncing on his white trainers. He stopped near them. None of them had masks on, but everyone was keeping a safe distance. The difference with his time in China, even in Moscow and London, was striking. Yes, some people wore face masks here, but it wasn't mandatory, and use seemed based on your likely politics.

"You should know, Rob, that when we meet with anyone outside our company, masks are mandatory." Bishop seemed to know what Rob had been thinking.

"OK," said Rob.

"Did you get the office protocol email?" said Bishop.

"Not yet," said Rob.

"You'll get one. We have a mandatory Coronavirus test every week when you come into the office. You'll have to do it before you can log in to any system. Faith should have told you about that."

Faith opened her mouth to say something, then closed it as Bishop continued.

"I expect Faith was distracted by the terrible graffiti on our building. It'll cost tens of thousands of dollars to have the front of the building returned to its pristine condition." He lowered his voice. "You do know these BLM people are being manipulated, don't you?" A look of disgust crossed his face.

"How's that?" said Rob. It sounded like a conspiracy theory to him.

"Their Facebook feeds and their Instagram and whatever else they are using are deliberately loaded with BLM posts, petitions, and images of police hitting protestors. Pictures of young girls being attacked by the police are shown to young men, and boys being beaten to young women. Some of the images are staged, some years old, but put a BLM label on it and young people will believe anything."

Rob shook his head slowly. "There is a real protest movement too," he said. "It's not all fake. The police can be trigger happy over here."

"They're protecting us, that's all," replied Bishop, swiftly. "We need the police to be firm or there'll be anarchy."

Rob's reply was just as quick. "You know people have a right to protest if that firmness becomes deadly and unjustified violence against black people."

"I've no problem with peaceful protest, but it's being fanned by people who want to manipulate us. This is real too, Dr. McNeil. These are the first large-scale, real-life manipulation tests in the United States. These programs have been going on for years, mostly just online. It's all one big psy-ops project. Just because manipulated posts never turn up in your feed doesn't mean it's not real. You know they can assemble demonstrators in any town or city in America in two hours! It's a real problem."

"Are we that easy to manipulate?" said Rob.

"Yes, we are. Most people don't believe the first such post they see, but after four or five we do. And it's not our government doing this."

"Who's doing it?"

"That's the sixty-four billion dollar question."

"This could impact the election," said Rob.

"That looks like the plan."

"Did you see that someone's leaving piles of bricks in the path of protesters?" Rob asked.

"There're people who want to tear this country apart and all they need are protests to start it all," said Faith.

There was silence for half a minute.

"You want me to do my virus test?" said Rob, changing the subject. Living in London had given him a different perspective on many things. He'd always tried to follow a middle ground. It was the path his mother had always advocated. But he had defended the United States many times in London, explaining how the US uplifted minorities, contradicting the biased views of some Europeans. He'd found out that changing people's minds on such things was not easy. So he'd learned to say his piece and move on.

"Yes, Dr. McNeil, for sure. We need to get it done before we head out to our main laboratory," said Bishop.

"Where's that?"

"Maryland, about an hour from here," said Bishop.

"We can get there in fifty minutes with the reduced traffic these days," said Faith.

"Where in Maryland?" said Rob.

"Just outside Frederick," said Bishop.

Rob's heart tightened. "At Fort Detrick?"

"Yep, we operate on Fort Detrick land. It helps with the security."

Rob had, of course, heard of Fort Detrick, the main United States biological weapons development and testing center since the second world war. There were rumors that Coronavirus strains had been enhanced there. He'd often wondered if he would end up working there.

A few people he knew had worked at Fort Detrick. They'd all been very positive about the place. The undercurrent in the conversations he'd had was always how you could take what you learned there and use it to help private enterprise make a killing.

"I've never been there," he said.

"Well, we won't be going to the main facility. They closed some of that a few years ago. But you will get a flavor of the place."

"They didn't close you down too?"

"No, we're totally separate."

"I heard there was a biological containment breach. Did that not affect you?"

"No, and the facilities there came fully back on line in April, just over a month ago," said Bishop. "We're delighted to see them all working again. There was never any real breach. It was a protocol issue. A misunderstanding. Someone at the CDC was being over-zealous."

Rob had heard about the incident. It was big news in the vaccine research community before the pandemic had changed everything.

"Weren't researchers from Fort Detrick also working on Coronavirus research on bats with Chinese researchers?" asked Rob.

"It was a small study. It's all stopped now by order of the president," said Bishop with a disinterested shrug. "I'll order a car to pick us up out front. Meet me down there after your test."

Faith took him to a small room with a green cross on the door. A woman in a full hazmat suit took a blood sample.

"Sit, five minutes, please," said the woman after taking some blood, gesturing toward some black plastic seats in a screened off waiting area. Rob went there but remained standing.

"Things are moving fast," said Rob, when the woman disappeared. Faith was standing just outside the seating area, checking her phone.

"There's a lot going on you don't know about," she said, keeping her head down.

"OK, but I've security clearance now. I'm a TOTALVACS employee," said Rob. "You can tell me anything."

"No, you're a partner employee," said Faith, with a shake of her head. "You have limited clearance."

"A trusted partner, I hope. And if you guys want help, you are going to have to open up a little about what's going on."

Faith looked up from her phone. She looked concerned. "We have a contamination problem, Rob. I can tell you that, because it's public information. I can also tell you that we don't know where it originates. That too is public information."

"Connecting the dots. That's why I'm here, right?" said Rob.

"And a lot more than that, too," said Faith.

The woman came back with his test results. They were on her smartphone.

"Open up your Bluetooth," she said.

Rob tapped at his phone. A Bluetooth request popped up. He accepted it. A TOTALVACS app appeared on his screen seconds later. When he opened it, a green circle showed he was clear of the virus.

"You're quick," he said.

"We have the fastest test in the world," she said, proudly.

"Let's go," said Faith. "We don't have a lot of time."

19

Washington DC, June 1ˢᵗ, 2020

Vladimir sat up straighter in the All Services vehicle two blocks from TOTALVACS. They had traced over a hundred vehicles exiting the building and had matched them to probable staff addresses, possible partner buildings, and other government locations.

The location that interested him most was the Wilshire Creek Condos. It was a known apartment complex Chinese Embassy staff used. The AI tracking system had also identified a vehicle coming from the Wilshire Creek complex and dropping someone off at TOTALVACS that morning.

The system was a serious step up from the local traffic management system, able to track the comings and goings at target locations and linking them together. Privacy advocates would be incensed if they knew what was happening, but what they didn't know couldn't annoy them.

This was the cutting edge of Russian state security software. Only FSB and some senior Russian government staff even knew it existed, though it was likely that the CIA was aware of the system and even had its own.

They very likely had spies inside the FSB.

He peered closer at the screen. The camera focused on the front of the TOTALVACS building showed a black

Chevy had pulled up. Vladimir let out a soft "Ha," when he saw who was coming out of the building.

Rob and Faith climbed into the waiting Chevy. It headed west toward George Washington Memorial Parkway.

"We need to follow them," said Vladimir, pointing after the vehicle. If they went outside the city, he would lose them on the DC vehicle tracking cameras.

The All Services vehicle Vladimir was in followed the Chevy at a good distance, at least four to five cars behind. After they reached the George Washington Memorial Parkway, they drove for about eight miles until the Chevy exited onto the I-495, and a few miles later, onto the I-270 heading into Maryland.

"Hold back," said Vladimir to the driver when they reached the I-270. If the driver of the Chevy was using standard procedures, he'd be watching for any vehicles that followed his highway exits.

And it didn't take a genius to work out where Rob and Faith were going. The FSB had also managed to tap into the traffic surveillance system around Fort Detrick only a year before. Vladimir would know, if they turned onto the US-40W, that that was where they were heading.

Tracking the movements of staff and visitors around Fort Detrick had been a Holy Grail for the FSB for decades.

Fort Detrick was where the CIA and the United States military experimented with mind-control, crop destruction, and all types of biological weapons. It was of interest to the Russian state what went on there. If Rob was involved with Fort Detrick, everything had changed. He'd heard a rumor in Moscow that Coronaviruses had not only been experimented on at Fort Detrick, but that someone had transported a batch to Wuhan for further gain-of-function

83

experiments to be carried out and that an accidental leak of that work, by the Chinese, had caused the current pandemic.

A lot of vaccine experiments had been moved to China, not just the ones that required human subjects, so it was plausible that it had escaped. Although there was an alternative theory that the release was not an accident.

If he found out any evidence of that, he was bound to report it immediately. Moscow would light up in excitement if he did.

Vladimir watched as the Chevy up ahead turned onto the US-40W.

"Don't follow them," he told the driver. He tapped at the keyboard. He had to find out more about what Dr. Robert McNeil was up to.

20

Maryland, June 1ˢᵗ, 2020

The traffic was moving fast. The pandemic had certainly done away with a lot of traffic jams.

"Clear behind," said the driver. He'd been watching his rearview mirror intently since they'd been on the I-95.

"Good," said Bishop. He was sitting up front with the driver. Faith and Rob were behind. Bishop had hardly spoken since they'd left K Street.

Fifteen minutes later they passed a sign saying Nallin Farm Gate, Fort Detrick. They didn't turn in. Rob sat quietly in the back.

A few minutes later, on a quiet part of the road, with a dense covering of oak hickory trees on either side, they pulled off the road and headed up a forest access path.

The path ended a minute later at the high black-mesh fence that headed away on each side into the trees. The Chevy stopped. The fence was topped with razor wire. A second fence lay behind it.

There was no guardhouse at the gate. They waited. Bishop tapped at his smartphone screen impatiently, as if summoning someone to open the gate ahead.

A buzzing noise, like a flock of bees, came from outside the Chevy. Rob looked around. At first, he thought a flock of birds had descended on them. Then he realized what it was. A swarm of micro-drones had surrounded their

85

vehicle. One hovered at each window. Each had a tiny camera lens pointing into the vehicle.

"This is up-to-date security," said Rob.

"They can disable a vehicle," said Bishop. "Make sure you smile for the camera."

With a rising hum, the swarm rose above them. The gate in front of them slid open.

They drove along the road, which twisted and turned up the side of a hill until finally, they pulled up at an entrance set into the hillside. The smoked glass door had the roots of a tree hanging above it. It looked like something from an alien movie.

Bishop turned to him. "Never speak about what you see here. Never write down your memories of this facility and especially never tell anyone close to you anything about this location."

"How will you know if I do?"

Bishop shook his head. "Trust me, we know everything. We know if you've ever visited a porn site since the internet was invented, what your political view is, how it's evolved, and every medical condition you ever looked up online. We know everything."

Faith nudged his arm. "Don't worry, I vouched for you. The State Department did a full internet history search with every ISP you've ever been registered with. There was nothing unusual. Except," she said and smiled, "you have a weird taste in movies."

Rob didn't smile back. He didn't care what they found out about him. What he wanted, was to know if they could help him. And surely, if they had all this data, they had to know the name of the person who'd invited him to Paris. Peter was just as likely not going to even bother emailing him what he knew. Early confirmation of who had lured him to Paris would be a very good thing.

"Let's go inside," said Bishop.

The door into the underground offices slid open as Bishop approached. Ahead was a long passage leading straight into the hill. A disinfecting station stood to the left. They sanitized their hands and put on white N-95 masks.

"Being underground helps avoid snoopers," said Bishop. They headed down the passage to a bank of three elevators. Bishop looked into an iris scanner. A silver elevator door on the left slid open and they went inside. The floor buttons were marked with a minus sign. They went down to minus five—the lowest level.

"The temperature and humidity are maintained at optimal levels here," said Bishop. "We're both energy neutral and off the grid."

Faith rolled her eyes.

"I want you to see the manufacturing facility first," said Bishop. "We're already working on your vaccine formula."

"You jumped the gun," said Rob. "We haven't even signed the papers yet." He adjusted his face mask at his ears.

"We won't start the trials without your agreement," said Bishop. "But we want to be ready to go as soon as possible after we do get your partners' agreement."

"Any news on that?" said Faith.

"It'll happen," said Rob.

"Yeah, I knew with your support it would go through," said Bishop.

They exited the elevator into a semi-circular reception area, like the one in the building in K Street. Bishop, Faith, and then Rob, all had their irises scanned and then a door in the far wall slid open.

Laurence O'Bryan

"You don't do clip-on badges here," said Rob. "Every government building I've ever visited used to hand them out like sweets."

Bishop stared up at a white camera pod in the roof. "We're all tracked from the moment we set foot in here. We don't need germ-carrying, easily forged badges."

"I wish every lab would go along with that," said Rob.

"They will. We have a patent on the human resource asset tracking system."

Bishop led the way down the corridor. Steel doors were set into white walls on both sides. The corridor was eerily empty. Their steps echoed.

"Access to this floor is tightly controlled," said Bishop. He stopped at a door. It also had an iris scanner. He leaned toward it. "Only the chosen few get in here," he said.

The door clicked open. They went inside to a long room with a window taking up all of the far wall. Bishop went to the window and looked into the giant room beyond.

Steel vats of various sizes, pipes, tubes, a steel manufacturing line, and testing tables were laid out in the room below. People in blue hazmat suits were walking around. They appeared to be checking things.

"We're ready to start manufacturing," said Bishop. "For this program, we won't wait for test results. We make it and use it all or throw it all away. It's the only way we can get the volume of vaccine we'll need to stop the virus."

21

Washington DC, June 1st, 2020

Wang Hu stepped out of the red Chinese Embassy Mercedes. It had been purchased to signal the excellent cooperation between the Federal Republic of Germany and the People's Republic of China. The color certainly meant that it was easy to spot.

The man he was meeting would be coming from the Senate Hart Building where he worked. Wang was dropped off on D Street NW. The walk through Lower Senate Park, with the Capitol Building on his right, would help him shake vehicles following him. He looked at his phone. Timing was everything with these missions. He had fifteen minutes to walk through the park and then back to reach the trash can at the corner of D Street at exactly noon.

He sat on a park bench and pulled out a plastic container with rice and vegetables and a plastic fork from the brown paper bag he had been carrying. He ate quickly, then relaxed on the bench, and put everything back in the paper bag.

The sun was beating down now. The park had a few joggers and other people heading to the Senate Hart Building, where there were always hearings or meetings going on, even in the middle of a pandemic. He'd been warned that there were far fewer people on the streets these days in Washington, which he meant he had to get this just right.

He headed for the trash can, scrunching his paper bag. As he reached it, a man in a gray suit passed by.

Wang dropped his paper bag in the trash can and picked up the postage-stamp-sized memory card that was sitting on the top of the trash can, as if he'd stumbled and was leaning out for support.

Twenty minutes later he was back at the embassy and uploading the data on the card.

It was encrypted, of course, but he had the digital key required to read the data. A few seconds later, data streamed onto his screen.

The list of names, dates, and active duty stations was long, containing the entire list of three hundred and thirty-six thousand, nine hundred and sixty-eight United States Navy active duty personnel.

He ordered the columns by command center and identified the information he was looking for: the number of personnel in each unit listed as exempt from duty because of a positive Coronavirus test.

22

Maryland, June 1st, 2020

"Can I assume the signed agreement will be with us today?" asked Bishop.

"You like jumping the gun, don't you?" replied Rob.

They were sitting in a meeting room near the observation area Bishop had taken them to.

"We have a situation, Dr. McNeil. We need to jump every gun."

"What situation?"

"There's a Coronavirus outbreak at a military location we need to stamp out. This is also an ideal location for part of the phase three test."

"Where is that?"

"I can't tell you. I'd have to confine you to this building for ninety days, maybe longer."

"Let me check my email." Rob pulled out his smartphone. The TOTALVACS app had apparently also logged him into the laboratory Wi-Fi. The system was fast too. There was an email from Sean Ryan.

The message said.

Rob,

Problem with the contract. They are looking for control of the manufacturing rights, specifically who chooses any manufacturing partners. We shouldn't give that away. Do you agree?

Also, we've received threats by email telling us to stop all vaccine research.

Sean.

Rob's finger paused over the screen as he thought about his reply. Under normal circumstances, he'd insist on having a say in where his vaccine was manufactured. But these were not normal circumstances. He had other priorities now.

Sean,

I need the contract signed today. We have a situation here and need to get the phase three trial underway. My vote is still to proceed. TOTALVACS knows what they are doing. And please, stop all research work until I get back.

Rob.

He sent the reply and looked up at Bishop. "You'll get the contract by tomorrow. You can press the start button on the manufacturing. But," he shook his hand in the air to emphasize his point, "I want to see all the trial's data and I will go public if the results are poor and the dangers to public health exceed the benefits."

Bishop shook his head. "You can't do that, ever. You've signed a non-disclosure agreement."

"So you can sue me."

Faith put a hand up. "Let's cross that bridge when we come to it. No point falling out over something that may never happen."

"Rob, take it from me, you don't want to cross us." Bishop leaned back in his chair.

"I am about to hand you control over something that's potentially worth billions of dollars, Dr. Bishop," said Rob, his voice raised. "I'll need access to the data and will consider it a breach of contract if you don't provide it."

Bishop just smiled in reply.

"And I need to find out who lured me to Paris."

"We're looking into it," said Faith.

"We are not your enemy, Rob," said Bishop. "There are a lot of lives at stake. Millions of lives. If this virus isn't controlled, we won't be talking about a hundred thousand deaths in the United States, we'll be talking about millions."

"I know," said Rob.

"The whole world is watching us," said Faith. "We should lead the world out of this."

"When I was there, the Chinese were bragging about how wonderfully they're doing controlling it," said Rob.

"We believe in personal freedoms," said Bishop. "They don't. I'd rather live free than have the state tell me what side of the bed to sleep on. They're also lying about what's really going on there." He leaned forward. "We're going to squeeze them, Rob. They've been playing us for fools. It's time they were taught a lesson. We're going to prove this vaccine works and some others too and show them democracy produces the goods."

Faith looked around. "You said there were manufacturing engineers who wanted to meet Rob," she said.

Bishop looked at his phone. "They'll be coming here in the next few minutes."

"What's the meeting for?" said Rob.

"You're going to spend the afternoon reviewing the vaccine manufacturing line they've set up," said Bishop.

"Thanks for letting me know in advance," said Rob.

"I just have," said Bishop.

A knock sounded from the door.

23

Virginia, June 1st, 2020

Wang looked at the online map. They were heading down the I-64 after passing Richmond. Norfolk was an hour away.

The traffic was busy, but there were no snarl ups. They would be in Ocean View within the hour. The naval station wasn't far. The work he had to do should not take long. The contact would arrive alone.

"Do we eat?" asked the driver.

Wang turned off his phone.

"No, we don't want cameras at rest stops picking up our mug shots when we go to the restrooms. You brought a bottle to piss in?"

"Yes," said the driver.

"We don't want anyone breathing down our necks."

"We're coming up to the Ocean View off-ramp. This is the turn, sir?" said the driver.

"Yes, head straight to the ocean, then turn right and park when you get to the Burger King."

"But don't go in, yes, I got it."

"I'll be gone about an hour. Stare at the ocean, my friend. It's relaxing. It's meditating. That's what they all do here in the United States now, right? You can do that too, yes?"

"Most certainly."

They pulled up a few minutes later. Wang slid the side door of the vehicle open. He crossed to the other side of the street and looked back. With its darkened side windows, few people would even see that there was someone waiting inside.

The house he was looking for was half a mile away on Hillside Drive; a newly painted, light-blue, shingle-fronted house with a white porch. It was the only one like that on the whole road, so he'd been told.

He walked on, found the house, walked up to it purposefully, as if he knew where he was going, and opened the front door, which was unlocked.

"Hello," he called out.

There was no answer.

The house was furnished in a minimalist style. He sat at the table in the kitchen and waited. He looked at his phone, checking it was still off. Then he looked at his watch. The contact would be here in ten minutes.

He had on two sets of disposable gloves. He took a pre-paid Mastercard out of the slim box it had been sitting in, in his pocket. He held it up to the light by the edges. It was impossible to see the thin coating that had been applied. He put the card down on the table and sat on the far side.

A few minutes later, the contact arrived. He was in civilian clothes. Like Wang, he had probably parked a good distance away. This was supposed to be a thank-you meeting; the pay-off meeting. He wouldn't want anything to be traced to him.

And it wouldn't.

The man had only one giveaway that he was part Chinese. His hair was pure black. Whether he'd carried out the work for nationalistic reasons or for money was still unclear.

Wang greeted him enthusiastically.

"Comrade, it a pleasure to finally meet you," he said, in Mandarin.

The man looked worried.

"The payment card for you is on the table. Twenty thousand dollars has been loaded on it and it's untraceable. You can use it almost anywhere."

The man picked it up, held it with both hands, turned it over.

"I can do more, if you want," he said.

"We'll call you. We think you've done enough for now," said Wang.

The man looked around, then licked a finger to get rid of something sticky. He put the card down. "Is this a set-up?" he asked.

"You're welcome to look around the house. There are no cameras, no FBI cybersecurity agents about to jump out, and no microphones." Wang opened his jacket, pulled his shirt up to show his lightly haired chest. "You did a great job. We are saying thank you, as we promised. That's all." Wang bowed a little, in a show of respect.

The man stood, looked into the next room.

"It's not that I don't trust you," he said. "But I'm going to have to check." He headed for the door to the pantry, then went upstairs. Wang could hear him clomping around the empty house.

Even if he left now, spooked by something, the residue on his fingers, which had made him lick at least one, should be enough for the purpose. Inducing a heart attack was the easiest way to get rid of someone without alerting the authorities. And for someone who'd triggered warnings that he was about to double cross them, it was an ideal way to go.

Wang smiled as the man came back into the room and picked up the card. He had a hand on his chest already.

"Until the next time," said Wang. He looked at his watch and headed for the front door. "Thank you deeply from the motherland," he said, as he opened the door. "You go first."

The man put his hand out to shake Wang's. Wang extended his elbow instead. The man tapped it and headed out into the street, one hand still at his chest, just over his heart.

He'd put the Mastercard into his wallet before he left. Wang went back inside and to the front window and watched as the man headed down the street. He'd make it to his car, possibly half-way home, before there'd be an accident. He'd collapse at the wheel. Hopefully, not too many other people would die, but one thing was sure, the man he'd met would be dead within an hour or at the most, two.

He exited the house, setting the lock to close after him. He would be on his way back to Washington in a few minutes. He headed in the opposite direction to the man he'd just met.

24

Washington DC, June 2ⁿᵈ, 2020

"We can't get out of it now," said Rob. "We need to be seen to be doing the right thing."

"Giving them exclusive manufacturing rights is way beyond our normal terms," said Sean.

"It's only for this exact variant of the vaccine. I expect there will be mutations and we'll be creating new vaccines each year, if not every few months, once the first success is under our belts. We can expand the manufacturing then."

"I'll agree, on that basis," said Sean.

Rob was in his room at the apartment complex. It was four in the morning, nine a.m. in London.

"Did Peter say anything about the invitation I received to go to Paris?" asked Rob.

"Nothing to me."

"There's something strange about that," said Rob.

"Are you sure you're not just being paranoid?" asked Sean.

"I'm sure."

"Were you in Wuhan in October last year?"

"No, mid-November," said Rob. "Why do you ask?"

"I saw a report that they closed that Wuhan Institute in mid-October and had road-blocks all around it."

"I missed that. They never said anything about it when I was there, which is what they're like in China. They hate to lose face. The facility in Wuhan is leaky, Sean. There's been a number of reports, some even reached the press. They won't open up their records for international inspection either. No chance."

"They're trying to blame the US."

Rob hesitated. He wasn't sure if this was the right time to say it, but he knew from Sean's interest in what was going on, and the history they had together, that he should tell him. And he needed to tell someone. He was still wondering himself if he'd done the right thing and it was starting to get to him.

"I'm also cooperating with a Chinese government official."

"What the hell?" said Sean, his voice exploding in Rob's ear.

"I'm a liaison person, that's all."

"What? You know they're trying to use you."

"Yeah."

"Be very careful, very, very careful."

Rob's stomach had tightened. "They want to know what's happening with our vaccine."

Sean laughed. "Them and everyone else. I had a call from the Prime Minister's office asking the same thing." He laughed again, louder. "I'm expecting one from the Queen any minute."

"Peter's probably looking for a Knighthood."

"Yeah, could be." There was a pause. "I trust you, Rob. You know that. Just get the job done."

"Thanks. I'll get back to you." Rob closed the line.

He trusted Sean. They'd been involved in a previous difficult situation about a vaccine. A big player had tried to

99

Laurence O'Bryan

buy them out to stop a vaccine from being released. Rob knew from that incident that Sean was more concerned about doing the right thing than piling up cash. It was why he stayed in the institute, despite getting offers from other labs.

Jackie had been proud of him then, and of the institute, when she'd heard about what had happened. "You are truly amazing," she'd said when he'd told her. He remembered it clearly. The smile on her face before she kissed him.

Millions of lives had been saved because of the institute's commitment to making low-cost vaccines made available to the poorest for free, those who need them most.

He didn't like to talk about it all, as there were a lot of cynics who'd assume he had an ulterior motive for everything he did.

Oh God, how he missed Jackie. It really felt as if parts of him—his arm, his heart, and half his brain—had died with her.

She'd helped him focus on his work, to enjoy the small things in life, to disregard setbacks.

It would be so good to be able to call her now.

It was getting bright outside. He decided to go for a walk in the nearby park. He dressed, put on his shoes. As he was about to open the door of his room, he heard voices in the corridor. His hand stopped above the door handle.

It was Jackie! What?

She was alive.

She was laughing with someone.

A hand reached in and grabbed his heart. The room became smaller, the walls closing in. A shout began in his chest.

He threw open the door.

Two women had passed by. One of them glanced back at him. Neither of them looked like Jackie.

The shout died in his throat. His gut tightened fast as an overwhelming feeling of foolishness rose up inside him.

He went out, closed the door behind him with a shaking hand, and headed for the park.

25

Vladimir shifted in his seat. The All Services vehicle was equipped for long surveillance operations. No one who peered in could see into the back, even if they came right up to the windscreen and peered in. A camp bed stood in a corner. That allowed a two-person team to take breaks.

Bottles and biscuit tins were used instead of a toilet. If it was an American stake-out unit they'd probably have a built-in chemical toilet, but this was not their country and they might have to abandon a vehicle if they were made. A half-assed surveillance set-up would look like local criminals. A vehicle with a chemical toilet and all the facilities of home could be a state operation.

The Wilshire Creek Condos complex was an ocher six-story row of apartment blocks on Connecticut Avenue, shielded by a row of American beech and elm trees. The nearby Malvin C. Hazen Park also boasted scarlet oak, cedar, and poplar trees.

The walking trail through the park ran down to the narrow Rock Creek river and then branched north and south along the creek.

Vladimir spotted Rob coming out of the condos at seven-fifteen. It was early enough that most of the walking crowd still hadn't arrived, but the serious joggers had. Rob headed west through the park toward the creek. Vladimir followed. Rob walked quickly and didn't look around.

The trail curved through trees and when it reached the creek, Rob turned around and headed back. He saw Vladimir when they were about fifty feet apart. He stopped and stared, his hands on his hips. Vladimir walked toward him, stopped six feet from him.

"What the hell are you doing in Washington?" said Rob.

"Keeping an eye on you, what else?" said Vladimir with a shrug. "We got on so well."

Rob shook his head. "What do you want?"

"I'll give it to you straight, as I know you like it that way," said Vladimir. "We'd like you to put a monkey in your vaccine wrench."

Rob shook guffawed loudly. "Are you crazy? You mean slow things down?"

"That would be good."

"Why?" Rob exploded. "Millions of people will die if we don't get a vaccine approved soon."

"You are working with TOTALVACS now, yes?" said Vladimir. "Did you know they're responsible for multiple botched vaccination programs?" he asked. "The whole anti-vax movement is based on their work."

"Really? That's news to me."

"Maybe, but it's all true. They were expelled from India for killing thousands with their vaccine tests."

"Maybe that was a long time ago. Testing standards have changed dramatically in the last few years."

A pair of joggers passed them by. They both looked studiously into the distance as they jogged.

Rob looked around, as if wondering who might be watching them. "How did you know where to find me?"

103

"We know more than you think."

"OK, great, and thanks for the warning about TOTALVACS. Now, I have to go," said Rob. He stepped to the side and started to pass Vladimir.

"What if I told you your wife isn't dead?" said Vladimir, softly. He looked around, his eyes darting.

Rob stopped, put a hand up, pointed directly into Vladimir's face. "Don't say that." His hand was shaking. His body tense.

Vladimir stepped back, looked at Rob's hand. He pulled a smartphone from his pocket, tapped at the screen, and turned it to Rob. A video started.

Rob's face went pale. He blinked rapidly. Was this for real?

26

Washington DC, June 2nd, 2020

Wang walked across the intersection at 23rd St. The traffic on the street was light. The Pan American Health Organization building occupied the entire triangular block ahead, sitting at the intersection with Virginia Avenue. The structure looked like a small United Nations building in New York with its row of flags and a circular building at the front—like a giant gray circular cushion with a ten-story office block looming behind.

He approached the main entrance. Multiple security camera systems were watching everyone who came and went. The interior of the building was regularly swept for spying devices. The extra fifty million dollars China had pledged to the World Health Organization, the parent organization of the Pan American Organization, ensured there was enough money for deep security, despite the United States having pulled out its funds.

He reached the glass main door and entered as a group from a South American country exited. He had a white N95 mask on. They had blue face masks on. This was one corner of Washington DC where proper health protocols were observed.

The woman at the reception desk took his name and asked him to wait while she called his contact. But even before he stepped back from the desk, he heard his name being called.

"Mr. Wang, it is good to see you," said a lilting voice in Mandarin.

He turned. Walking toward him was a memory. A stab of regret pushed up inside him. Seeing Ms. Gong Dao in all her glory always gave him that feeling.

Gong was slim, tall, and wearing a black face mask. Her eyes smiled at him. The black suit she wore was an inch too tight, and the skirt an inch too short for someone of her status. Half the men in the Washington office were probably in love with her. Half the women probably hated her for that. The others probably wanted to be her.

Gong's bow was almost imperceptible. Wang's replying bow less so.

"Please, follow me," said Gong.

She led the way to an elevator, with most of the men in the reception area following her with their gaze.

She pressed a button, turned to Wang as the elevator doors closed. She raised her hand, as if he might kiss it. As his hand came up to hers, she pulled hers away.

"I forgot. We must not touch," said Gong, in a wistful tone.

Wang's hand, as if it had been pulled up by a string, now broken, dropped away. He was glad he'd cajoled his way to Washington. The most precious jewel of the Chinese Communist Party worked here.

Gong led him down a narrow corridor with doors on each side. She stopped at a table with hand sanitizer bottles on it, poured some on her hands and on his, and opened a door with her elbow. The meeting room had a view over the city with the spike of the Washington Monument visible in the distance above the trees, between two dark, brick-like office blocks between them and the city center.

Gong went to the window, looked out.

"Did you ever imagine we'd end up here?" said Gong.

Wang stood behind her. He breathed in the lemony smell of her hair. Memories flooded back of his younger self, his enthusiasm for the party, their energetic lovemaking in his tiny student room in Beijing, and their efforts to be quiet so that he wasn't thrown out of the building in the middle of the night. But most of all, he remembered his naivety.

They'd promised they'd stay together forever, but at the first chance of a foreign promotion, she'd gone. Their long-distance affair had petered out as he rose up the ranks in Beijing and offers of female comfort came his way.

But he'd never forgotten her. And the two times he'd seen her in the last few years had been the highlights of each year.

"Why are you here?" asked Gong.

"You must do more," said Wang, enjoying the moment, the little bit of power he had over her.

"Such as?"

"There must be no public criticism of the People's Republic of China. You are simply on assignment at the Pan American Health Organization. I hope I do not have to remind you that you still work for our embassy. Number two, we will set the terms for any investigation into events at Wuhan. Make that clear to everyone here." He paused, transfixed by the downy hairs on her neck. If he blew hard, they would move. He remembered doing that.

She shifted on her feet, moving away from him. "And number three?"

"Recordings of all internal meetings discussing the Coronavirus this January must be deleted."

"That won't be easy." Gong turned to him. Her eyes were wide. Did he see in them an echo of her desire for him?

"It will be hard, yes," he said. He had to stop himself from leaning forward and reaching for her.

Gong narrowed her eyes.

"I'm getting married," she said, bluntly.

He blinked, forced his expression to harden.

"Who is the man?"

"You don't know him." She reached up, as if she would touch his face, then pulled her hand away.

"Someone who can help you, I expect."

She took a step toward him. "You could have followed me here."

A muscle tightened inside his chest, restricting his windpipe. He pressed his lips together.

"I have my career. Personal feelings cannot get in the way." His head shook with the force of his reply. "That is what the party teaches us."

She looked away. "You are still the same, Wang."

"Yes, I believe in the party. And now more than ever. The United States must be forced to its knees."

"How will we do that? Tell me."

"An explosion in Coronavirus cases is coming in a few weeks. The seeds have been sown."

"How many will die?" Gong looked into his eyes.

Wang felt himself weaken. He blinked, shrugged.

"And what will the contribution by Beijing to the WHO be?" Gong asked, softly.

"It will go up. It is a gesture to thank everyone here for their hard work."

She took another step closer to him. "There is something you can do for me, Mr. Wang."

Wang's cheek jerked. It was a spasm he occasionally got when he was stressed.

"What can I do for you?" he said. At the back of his mind, he was hoping she would offer herself to him.

"Tell your friends back in Beijing that they must hide our opioid exports to the United States better. I'm getting pressure from a variety of sources to do something about it," said Gong Dao.

Wang laughed, waved his hands about. "I will pass on your message, but I know what the response will be. This is how capitalism works. We meet demand. If we don't manufacture opioids, the Indians will. Tell anyone who complains that the Americans must curtail demand." He put his hand to his head, then pulled it away in a surprised gesture. "This is just an example of the much talked about freedom in the United States. Freedom to kill yourself with opioids."

Wang pointed toward the Washington Monument. "See, some very free protesters have started another fire."

A thin black column of smoke rose in the distance.

"And another?" said Wang. He pointed a little to the east.

Gong Dao nodded.

"This reminds me of Hong Kong last year, before we put our foot down," he said.

"You were there?" said Gong. She smiled at him.

"Yes, they needed some help."

"Interrogations?"

Wang didn't reply. He was looking at the gold Gaara Chinese love symbol dangling on a thin necklace around her neck. An urge to rip it from her boiled inside him.

109

Laurence O'Bryan

"What is the matter, Mr. Wang?" asked Gong.

He forced his feelings away, clasped both hands behind his back.

"Nothing is the matter," he said. "We will proceed with haste to our destination. That is all that matters."

"There is one small final thing," said Gong. She leaned close to him.

He could smell charcoal toothpaste on her breath.

"What?"

"I recommend we keep one recording from an internal World Health Organization discussion about the Coronavirus from mid-January."

"What does it show?" said Wang.

"I will send you a copy. Is there anything else, Mr. Wang?"

He was sorely tempted to tell her what he was thinking, but instead, he thanked her and allowed her to accompany him down to the main reception hall.

As he waited for the embassy car to arrive at the side of the building, he had a strange empty feeling, as if he had let something important slip from his grasp.

When he arrived back at the embassy, the video file was waiting in his inbox. It had been decrypted automatically. He turned in his chair, checking to see if anyone in the room allocated to visiting officials from Beijing was watching him. There wasn't. He started the video.

It looked like any other meeting video. First there were brief introductions, with people giving their names. Then he stopped the video. The next person on the screen was an American senator. He'd seen him on TV.

He plugged a set of earphones into the laptop. In his ears, the senator spoke. He had a youthful southern drawl.

"Ya'll know that if we delay the announcement of human to human airborne transmission for another week, the spread of this new virus will be hard to stop."

The camera switched to Gong Dao. "We cannot confirm airborne transmission until Beijing agrees," she said.

The screen switched back to the senator. Underneath him, the words *Senator Harmforth* appeared.

"I have to tell you; if you delay, you can be accused of deliberately allowing the virus to spread."

Gong Dao shook her head. "No government would dare do that." She leaned forward.

"We must wait for the approval of Beijing," said Gong Dao. "If you wish to raise an objection, it can be noted in the minutes, Senator Harmforth?"

"Ya'll go ahead with your plan," he said. "I am sure the White House will be ready to deal with whatever happens over here."

Wang checked the senator's website to see if he had engagements in Washington. He discovered that Harmforth sat on an appropriations committee meeting that day.

Wang saved the video and attached a text overlay with the meeting date—10th of January 2020—and placed the clip in a password protected area of Nutstore. Few in the United States used the Chinese version of Dropbox, but Senator Harmforth would figure out how to access it when he received the email.

He composed it and sent the link, a screen grab, and part transcript to the senator from a United States-based Gmail account.

From a friend. I have the full video of this meeting. I do not want it to get out to the media. Meet me at the main visitor entrance to the Capitol Building at nine tomorrow

111

morning. Wait twenty feet from the door. I will find you. I will offer you green tea.

He sent the message through a virtual private network that would hide where it came from. The party's virtual network was the highest grade encrypted-network in the world. It would take the United States a million years, using every computer in the country, to crack its decryption code.

27

Jackie was smiling, looking beyond the camera, as if someone was telling her what to do.

Rob's heart beat like a kettledrum. His knees went weak. He straightened, put a fist out, shook it toward Vladimir.

"What the hell is this? Some sick—"

Before he could finish, Jackie was speaking on the video he was watching. "Rob, do whatever Vladimir asks." The audio crackled. Then the video stopped.

"You bastard," said Rob. He took a step toward Vladimir, his fist up. "Where is she?"

They were toe to toe, with no masks on. Rob's breathing was coming fast. A deep tremble ran through him. Sweat ran from his brow.

"Answer me!" he shouted.

Vladimir smiled.

A young woman jogging toward them veered off into the trees.

"I do not know where she is," said Vladimir. He put his arms out wide. "That is the way it is in my country. They don't tell us things. That way, it doesn't matter if you beat me to a pulp and threaten to bury me in the woods. I still can't tell you anything." He let out a cynical laugh.

113

"OK, where did you get this video?" Rob was shaking. His eyes started to water. He blinked it all away, thrust his fist forward. His chest had tightened as if a band had been placed around it.

"It was sent to me." Vladimir sounded nonchalant.

"By who?" Rob shouted.

Two more joggers veered away from them.

"I will ask the questions from this point," said Vladimir, jutting his jaw out, his expression hardening.

Rob looked over Vladimir's shoulder, then stepped closer to him. As Vladimir's gaze shifted, he grabbed Vladimir's neck. The skin felt warm and rubbery under the collar of his shirt.

Vladimir just stood there. "Let go of me or my friend will put a bullet in your head."

"What friend?"

"To your left."

Rob turned his head. Among the trees stood a man with a black hoodie pulled up. He was carrying a dark jacket over his arm. The arm was pointed at him.

"I don't care," said Rob, anger in each word. "Where is my wife?"

"I honestly don't know. Getting yourself killed is not going to save her."

Rob growled, then released his grip.

"Never touch me again," said Vladimir, his voice tense.

"What do you want from me?"

"Has TOTALVACS started production of your vaccine?"

Rob nodded.

"Tell them to stop. Tell them you need to change the antigen formula." Vladimir's eyes narrowed. "Tell them you want to extend the period of immunity the vaccine will give."

Rob shook his head. "They won't buy that. This is bull crap. Are you telling me I can't get my wife back if I don't do this?"

"I am passing on a message. That is all. Do not blame the messenger."

Rob snorted in frustration. "How do I know she's alive? This could be some video trick."

"Have you ever seen a video like this of her?" Vladimir looked puzzled, as if he too was wondering if the video was real.

"No."

"Then I suggest you do what I requested. What is a few weeks' delay in your vaccine? It will be a better one this way. What's the problem?" He smiled, but with his lips only, as if he thought Rob was stupid.

"And"—Vladimir leaned forward—"please, don't tell your friends in the American intelligence services anything about this. We know about your chats with Dr. Bishop. I will find out if you talk and we will not meet again."

Vladimir stepped back. "See you back here tomorrow morning, Dr. McNeil. I hope to have another video for you then. And"—he shook his head slowly—"do not follow me if you want to see your Jackie again."

28

Senator Harmforth put his phone to his ear. He listened as he walked along the corridor outside the senator's restaurant in the bowels of the Capitol building.

He nodded at senators and staffers passing by. Some had a face mask on, others didn't. The crowd was a lot thinner than on a normal Tuesday. The only senators still in the building were on committees and a few others who always did as they chose.

"Don't be like that, honey," he said. "You know I only met that Gong Dao to get information out of her. Trust me."

He lifted the phone away from his ear as the response came. He waited, then replied, "McNeil's wife had to be silenced, that was what happened to her."

"It's fake news," he said. "Someone's out to get me. Why don't you check your sources?"

29

Washington DC, June 2nd, 2020

"What happened to you, Rob?" asked Faith. They were in the TOTALVACS building in K Street. He had just spent the last five minutes insisting he needed to see Bishop.

"Nothing," he said. "I just realized we can improve the vaccine formula significantly."

They were sitting in one of the small meeting rooms overlooking the back of the building and a row of other office blocks, which blocked out the sun.

Faith did a double take. "Rob, you can't be serious. They've started the manufacturing process already."

"Well, they shouldn't have. I haven't sent them the signed agreement to start yet."

Faith let out a low gasp. "You were told they were going to start. You gave your word that you'd get the agreement signed."

"Are we going to do this the right way or the TOTALVACS way?" said Rob.

"The right way." Faith's cheeks were red.

"Look, I don't want to have to go public with my objections to the formula they will use for this phase three trial, but I will if I have to."

He leaned back. "You do know if there's an internal scientific objection that the trials cannot proceed."

"They can proceed, but FDA approval for the vaccine may be delayed while they investigate your objection."

"Is that what you want?" said Rob.

"No," said Faith.

"Well, either you delay now, or I'll get a delay at the end, Faith. I'm not changing my mind on this."

"What's going on, Rob? How come you're dropping this on us now?" She had a curious expression on her face.

"I just want to make sure the vaccine works." Rob sat up straight. He couldn't give anything away concerning his hopes about Jackie being alive.

At first, after Vladimir had gone, he'd dismissed the whole thing as an obvious set-up. The Russians probably had video systems that could replicate what someone looked like and get them to say anything.

Then, he'd remembered that the red top she was wearing in the video had only arrived from an online store the day before he'd gone to Paris.

How could they know that?

The video had to be real. She was alive. Thank God.

His fingers jumping about in excitement, he'd composed an email to Bishop outlining his reasons for wanting a delay for the vaccine. Then he sent it off. He'd received no reply.

So he'd come for the previously agreed meeting at ten that morning at TOTALVACS, expecting Bishop to be here and asking him detailed questions about his email, but only Faith had met him, and she didn't seem to know about his email at all.

"Has anyone been in contact with you?" Faith asked.

"Lots of people contact me. I get hundreds of emails every day."

"Has anyone tried to influence you?"

He stared straight ahead.

"Did you sleep well last night?"

"Sure."

"You went for a run early this morning."

"I went for a walk to clear my head."

"I'm just wondering where this sudden change of mind came from, Rob."

Now he knew. She'd been assigned to find out what had happened to him to make him send the email.

"Listen, Faith, I'm not joking. I will leave here now and contact the Federal Drug Administration with my objections to this trial. The FDA has the power to make an order stopping any trial." He leaned forward. "I bet TOTALVACS hasn't even completed the paperwork for the trial. I know everything's at warp speed for these vaccine trails, but if there's an objection from someone involved in the project, the whole thing has to stop."

"You won't do that, Rob. Your future as a vaccine scientist is on the line here. If you object to this phase three trial, which you agreed to only a few days ago, no one will ever invest in you or trust you again." She put her elbows on the table.

"We've been in contact with your partners at the Institute of Applied Research. They have no knowledge of any change to your vaccine formula."

"I bet you spoke to Peter Fitzgerald," said Rob. "Hold on."

He pulled out his smartphone and went into his email. Yes, there it was, an email from Peter. He opened it.

Rob,

Good news. I've found out the name of the person who recommended you for the talk in Paris. It was someone at the Pan American Health Organization called Gong Dao.

I hope this helps.

Also, I got an email from someone at TOTALVACS asking if there were any amendments to your vaccine formula being considered. I told them there weren't. I am sure you don't want to delay things at that end.

You're welcome,

Peter Fitzgerald.

Rob felt cold inside. Gong Dao had recommended him for the talk in Paris and had visited his wife. He looked up. "Fitzgerald knows nothing about the latest results from the phase two trials. The changes I'm recommending are to be made for good reasons."

"What phase two results? We thought they weren't in yet. Isn't phase three going to run in parallel with phase two and with the manufacturing?" Faith bit her lip. She looked concerned. She was a good actor.

"If you provide evidence, Rob, I am sure Bishop will agree to a change in schedule. But he'll need evidence."

"You'll get it," he said. He stood and headed for the door. He had to get out of the room. He had to think.

"You won't stay for coffee?"

"I need to prepare a report for Bishop."

"You can do that here."

"No thanks."

He went out the door. She didn't follow him. He was a big fat fly in their ointment now. If he stayed at one of their desks, using their Wi-Fi, they'd probably by tracking every key stroke he made and screen grabbing what he was doing every few seconds.

He headed for the street. He looked around when he got there. There were only a few people walking by, but no one paid him any attention. A yellow cab waited at the curb, but he figured that would be a State Department plant. Faith had probably ordered it up from the meeting room. He headed east along K Street and at the next intersection waited until he saw an empty yellow cab and hailed it.

He gave the Wilshire Creek Condos' address and sat back.

He had to get them to postpone the trials. The news that Gong Dao had been involved in getting him to Paris made Vladimir's revelation all the more believable. Everything about Jackie's death stunk to high heaven. He had to focus on getting Jackie released.

The immediate question was, should he make contact with the FDA and put in an objection now? He asked the driver to wait when he saw an open Subway, went inside, and ordered a meatball sandwich and a coke. He got it to go. He planned to work all afternoon. He'd need something to keep himself going.

He reached his room at the condo complex at twelve-thirty. He was writing his report for Bishop five minutes later. The excuse he would give would be real. He planned an amendment to the vaccine that would make it more suitable for poorer countries.

They could include a synthetic nanoparticle DNA wrapper to encourage an enhanced T-cell response, which would lead to a longer period of immunity for those who took the vaccine. This would also allow the vaccine to be delivered using an air-jet injection system which forces a vaccine through the top layer of skin using a burst of pressurized air.

Poorer countries would also not need refrigeration with the new formula. That would make it far less costly to deliver in the field. The benefits were real. Bishop could not ignore his recommendations. The FDA would have to intervene if Bishop was too short-sighted to do the right thing.

Rob was halfway through the report in thirty minutes. He was considering what Bishop's objections might be. Maybe he'd say it was impossible to create this type of synthetic DNA wrapper. He bent over his laptop. He'd remembered there was a scientific paper on the subject. He needed to find it.

His phone buzzed. Then it stopped. A US number.

It buzzed again. He clicked the answer button.

"Outside," said a voice with a hint of a Chinese accent.

Was that Wang? He decided to ignore the summons. Wang could come to him. He wasn't a puppet. Rob bent over his laptop. He needed a second scientific paper on the subject, to prove without doubt that what he was suggesting could be done.

He searched online. Then he ate his Subway sandwich. As he was finishing it, a knock sounded on his door. He looked through the spy hole.

It was Wang. He had his smartphone in his hand. He knocked again, but harder.

Rob opened the door. "Come in," he said. "No need to break the door down."

Wang came halfway in, looked around, put a finger to his lips. "Come with me, it's important," he said. He headed down the corridor. Rob thought for a moment, then grabbed his door card and followed. Wang could help, even if only as a distraction for Bishop.

Wang was a little ahead.

"Do you think every room here is bugged?" he said, loudly.

Wang just kept going.

Rob stopped at the glass door that led out into the garden at the side of the building.

"We can go out this way," he called after Wang. He pushed the door open, waited for Wang, then when he saw him coming back, he went out into the narrow garden between two of the apartment blocks. He spotted a wooden seat.

"Let's sit," he said. "I hope this is important. I've got a lot to do."

Wang sat, crouched over his phone. "You need to see this," he said. He turned his smartphone screen to Rob.

Rob sat down, but not close to Wang. A disturbance hung in the air around Wang, a malevolence that made Rob's skin crawl.

He looked warily at the screen. Someone was speaking at a meeting. It looked like an American politician he vaguely remembered. The man spoke about letting the White House deal with whatever happens.

"Why are you showing me this?"

"Do you see the date on the clip?" said Wang.

"Sure, January 10th."

Wang pulled the phone away. "What this proves," he said. "Is that politicians in the United States were aware of human to human airborne transmission of the Coronavirus in early January." Wang was agitated, his hands moving through the air.

"Your country could have closed down a lot sooner, but your partisan system, with each side blaming the other for dirty tricks, meant you spoke with many voices, all with

123

Laurence O'Bryan

a different opinion of the importance of this news about human to human transmission."

Rob shook his head. "That's just one person. And anyhow, I'd rather live in a place where I'm free to express my opinion, than one where my mouth is taped shut by the state."

Wang stood. "I'm trying to help you, Dr. McNeil. You need to know the truth about your own government."

"Sure, and you don't want to talk about how it all started." He took a deep breath, holding himself back. "Have you found out who sent Gong Dao to my house in London?"

"I am working on that." Wang slipped his phone into his pocket.

"And I gave your stupid clock to my contact at the State Department."

"Good, they know we are connected." Wang looked pleased. "How is your friend Faith these days?" he said.

"Why?"

Wang's expression changed to a look of mock concern.

"This video is not good news for your friend," said Wang, shaking his head.

"Go on."

"The senator in this video is the man she is planning to marry. The real issue is, how much did he tell her, and how much did your State Department know about human to human airborne transmission of Coronavirus all the way back in January?" He pointed at Rob. "Your government could definitely have saved a lot of lives if they had acted quicker and with an iron fist."

Rob shook his head. "Yeah right, and Mao was great at organizing things too with the iron fist that crushed millions. You lot haven't changed. No respect for individual human freedom or human life."

"What a wonderful thing you give your people— freedom and death." Wang sounded bitter. He turned and walked away from Rob.

Rob headed back to his room. Did he even care that the State Department know about how deadly the Coronavirus could be in January? Did it matter who Faith was marrying?

There was only one thing that mattered. Finding Jackie and figuring out what he could do to get her released.

He barely slept that night. Twice he had his phone in his hand and was about to call Faith, to tell her what he'd found out, but also to talk to her, to share what he'd been told about Jackie. The State Department might even help him get Jackie back.

But twice he put his phone away. The State Department might also enrage Vladimir, possibly have him questioned, which would be a waste of time as he probably had diplomatic immunity. But it might all stop him from helping Jackie.

30

"Who did you tell?" were the first words Vladimir asked him the following morning in the park. They were at the same spot at the same time. More joggers were active this morning.

Rob started walking. "No one. Let's keep moving," he said.

Vladimir followed him.

"Where are we going?" he asked.

"This trail circles around. We're not going anywhere," said Rob. He raised his voice. "Do you know where Jackie is? Can I talk to her?" he asked, his need clear in his voice.

"I still don't know any more than you," said Vladimir.

Rob stopped. His body shook with anger.

"Don't give me this bullshit. You showed me a video of my wife alive yesterday. She's supposed to be dead. Where is she?" His hands were fists by his side.

Vladimir looked at him, sighed. "I only get told what I need to know. They don't tell me everything."

"What the hell does that mean?"

"I do not know where your wife is, understood? I too thought she was dead until yesterday. This video arrived in my inbox. That's it."

126

"Who sent it to you?"

"This I cannot tell you."

"What, it's classified? Are you trying to torture me?"

"Wake up, Dr. McNeil," said Vladimir, forcefully. "You must simply do as we ask, if you want to see her."

"You have to prove she's alive first. Prove that this isn't some grotesque trick. You people are well capable of it."

"Us, using tricks? Your government is the master of all that. Do you want me to make a list for you?"

"If I don't see her, talk to her, I'm going to assume you are playing games with me," said Rob. He stepped back.

"I will ask if that can be done," said Vladimir. "I will make contact with you again. Have you kept your side of the deal? Have you stopped the manufacture of the vaccine?"

"I've told them we must stop the process to improve the vaccine. I've requested it. I am doing what you asked."

"And they have agreed?"

"Not yet, but I've threatened to report them to the FDA."

Vladimir nodded. "Good. You can also tell your TOTALVACS friends they should stop using those Chinese swab tests to see if someone is a carrier."

"What?"

"Fifty percent of the positives from those tests are false. You might as well toss a coin."

"You're spreading fake news, right?" said Rob. "What is it, some Russian company wants the contract?"

Vladimir's face was like granite.

"I'm meeting the TOTALVACS people in two hours. If you want me to push hard to get our vaccine

127

stopped, I suggest you prove to me that my wife is alive."
He took another step back.

"Ask yourself this," said Vladimir. "After she died,
did you see her body, or did they just show you a video?"

"I want to speak to her." He spat the words out, then
turned, walked away. His mind buzzed with questions. Was
Vladimir telling the truth? Could he get to speak to her? Or
was this all some sick Russian doll game, where every time
he got an answer, it just turned out to reveal another
question?

His stomach tightened again. What the hell was he
going to do?

A car was due to pick him up in an hour and take
him to TOTALVACS. He'd submitted his paper, but he
knew he'd probably have to make good on his threat to
complain to the FDA to make TOTALVACS stop
production. Bishop was no pushover.

He showered, stayed under the warm water trying to
clear his head. As he was finishing, he heard his phone
buzzing. He stepped out and tapped at the screen, water
running everywhere. It was a UK number.

"Rob," said Sean. "What the hell are you up to? That
guy Bishop wants me to overrule you and get permission to
proceed with manufacture. What's going on?"

Rob explained to him about the new formula and the
benefits it would bring.

"We'll be the only ones with a formula that most of
the world can afford, Sean," said Rob. He could sense he
sounded all wrong.

"That's not the priority for TOTALVACS."

"Well, it should be."

"Is there anything else behind this?" said Sean, suspicion in his voice.

Rob hesitated. It would be good to get Sean's input on Jackie still being alive. The urge to tell Sean about the video and that he was waiting to find out the truth was strong. He had the words ready in his mouth. But no, he couldn't. Not now, maybe later. He needed this line to be free.

"You know you can share anything with me," said Sean. "We've been through a lot, the two of us. Do you remember when I—"

Rob's phone buzzed. Someone else was trying to call him.

"I have to go, sorry, Sean. I have another call," said Rob. He tapped at this screen.

Be Jackie, come on, be Jackie.

31

Wang walked past the main visitor entrance at the back of the Capitol building. It was one minute to nine. He put his phone to his ear and ignored the occasional person passing. He'd been here before and there'd been lines outside. Not now.

"What did you find out?" he asked in Mandarin.

"Target stayed at The Ritz-Carlton last night," came the reply in clipped Mandarin.

"Room?"

"342."

"Who was with her?"

"A man."

He cut the call.

Senator Harmforth paced up and down, not far away. Wang walked toward him.

"Do you like green tea?" Wang asked, as he came near.

"Do not try to blackmail me," said Harmforth, his eyes blazing, his tone angry. "I'll have you arrested, and the key thrown away."

Behind Harmforth two young men, both of them bulging out of their black suits, had appeared.

Wang raised his hands. "This is not blackmail, Senator. We are all on the same side," said Wang. "My job

130

is to protect the good relationship between the People's Republic of China and the United States of America."

"You work for the Chinese Embassy?" said Harmforth.

"With full diplomatic immunity," said Wang with a thin smile.

Harmforth's face was puce now. "What the hell do you commies want now. Haven't you done enough damage?"

"You have this the wrong way around," said Wang. "You could have saved many, many lives if the United States had acted in January."

"What is it you want?"

"What we want is in both our interests, Senator. We have a symbiotic relationship, yes? Let us not be cutting off our noses to spite our faces."

"You lot are parasites, feeding off our great country," said Harmforth.

"And your greatest enterprises feed off the profits they make in our country from our workers," said Wang.

"I really don't get it," said Harmforth. He glanced around. A few people were staring at them. "Let's walk this way." He headed around the Capitol.

Wang kept pace with him. "Senator, we have one goal. To maintain the peace of heaven between us."

"Go on, get to it," said Harmforth. "You guys sure love beating all over the bush."

"We seek to support the World Health Organization, Senator." Wang put a hand on his chest. "Our support and guidance for the WHO is a symbol of our support for health everywhere in the world, for all people. Now, we want to enhance its decision-making powers with some new rules and voting arrangements. Your support will be appreciated in this."

"You can take your appreciation and shove it where the sun don't shine, commie." Harmforth's face contorted. A vein pulsed on his forehead. "You want to take the WHO and turn it into a commie propaganda tool? Well, if that's what you're up to, don't expect the United States to tag along. And, don't bother me ever again with threatening texts, if you don't want to feel my fist in your face, commie bastard."

He turned and walked away.

32

Washington DC, June 3rd, 2020

Rob's mouth opened. A Facebook messenger video call had started. His smartphone screen flickered as if his Wi-Fi had a poor signal. He stood.

"Jackie." His voice trembled with both hope and joy.

Jackie opened her mouth and spoke. No words reached him. She waved.

"I can't hear you," he shouted. His neck muscles tightened. His throat went dry.

On the screen, Jackie leaned forward. She looked concerned. But the picture was blurry. He moved his phone closer to his eyes. Her mouth had moved weirdly, as if the video signal had been interrupted.

Rob blinked. The screen went black and then she was back.

What could he ask her that no one else would know? His heart lifted as he looked at her, the chains of loneliness and grief that had bound him dissolving in a flood of relief.

"What result did you get to the test?" he asked, hopefully.

Jackie squinted, leaned forward, as if to catch what he'd said. "I have my medicine," she said. Her voice crackled, then the screen flickered and went black. This time it stayed that way.

"What?" screamed Rob. He tapped at the screen, tried to reconnect. Nothing happened.

She had to be alive. How could a fake be talking about medicine?

He grabbed his keycard and headed for the reception area, half running, to see if the Wi-Fi was better there. All the time he was tapping at his screen. A group of men passed him. None of them had face masks on. They looked at him as if he were crazy. Someone must have cracked a joke about him after he'd passed, as laughter followed him down the corridor.

He turned and raised a finger to them. When he reached the reception, the Wi-Fi signal was worse there. He wanted to throw his phone at the wall.

A young Chinese girl passed him, smiled, then paused with a worried look on her face.

"You OK, mister?"

He nodded, turned away, headed back to his room, walking fast, glancing behind to see if she was following him. She wasn't.

His chest itched now. His whole body felt hot. What the hell was going on. Was Jackie really alive? She had to be. He'd seen her. Back in his room, he leaned his head against the inside of the door, anguish gripping at him. Would Vladimir's bosses pull such a cruel stunt?

His phone buzzed.

It was Faith.

"The car's waiting for you," she said.

"I need to talk to you," he said.

"We have a meeting with Bishop as soon as you get here." Her voice slowed. "Are you OK? What do you want to talk about?"

"A change in plans."

It was time to take control.

33

"Where are we going, sir?" asked the young Chinese driver. He'd been driving around near the Capitol, slowly, waiting for a summons from Wang.

"The Ritz-Carlton in Georgetown." Wang was in the back of one of the Mercedes AMG SLs the embassy used for ferrying visitors around. He pressed his fingers into the black leather armrest. The senator's retribution would not come quick enough.

The car slid through the traffic.

"We head north first," said the driver. "There's a shorter route, but we've been warned to stay away from the city center. Is that OK, sir?"

"Yes," said Wang. "Fast as you can." He was thinking about Gong Dao now. Would she still be in the hotel room? He looked at his watch. Nine-thirty. If her mission last night was official, she'd still be in the room, as she'd be allowed to take some personal time after her job was finished.

If it wasn't official, if she was doing it for the yellow dragons, she'd be gone already. If she'd been a honey trap, there had to be a possibility he could win her back. His lucky day might be here.

If she'd spent the night with an American, for pleasure or for the yellow dragons, she would have put

136

herself in a difficult position. He smiled to himself, warmth coursing through him. This leverage might be enough to get her to bend.

Literally. As she used to do for him.

"Hurry, driver," he said. He snapped his fingers. "Get me there quick. Come on. Fast."

But every traffic light was red, and twice they got stuck behind a car with a family inside, moving at a snail's pace. He wanted to scream at the driver, but he knew from experience that might have the opposite effect. One driver he'd raged at had broken down in tears, another had crashed. He'd ended up in a street cab and late for a meeting.

He closed his eyes, breathed in. He pictured her in the bed in the hotel room, half asleep when she answered his knock at the door. He kept his eyes closed day-dreaming until the driver said, "Will you be needing me after the hotel?"

"Yes, wait nearby. I will call you." Wang looked out the window. The traffic was light. They would be in Georgetown soon. He should go back to the embassy within the hour. The head of security would be waiting for a report.

Wang was required to inform the man if he was in contact with politicians, cultural figures, or business leaders while in Washington. He wasn't required to tell him about waitresses he talked to, but he had to know about his meeting with the senator. It had to be reported.

What to put in the report was the easy part. As little as possible. The senator's rudeness would be mentioned, but not Wang's request for assistance with the proposed changes at the WHO.

Beijing was behind that. They would not want it revealed to the embassy until the mission was successful. There would be a loss of face if he revealed what his masters in Beijing wanted, if the senator refused and the objective was not achieved.

The hope was that the senator had blustered publicly but would comply when the moment of truth, a vote on a WHO committee, came about.

If the senator used Wang's intervention to suggest to the White House that the United States leave the WHO, that might be an even better outcome. Beijing would be in the driving seat. Wang smiled, breathed in slowly.

If the United States pulled out of the WHO, he would probably get another medal. What would they give him next?

"We are here, sir," said the driver, as they pulled up into the curved drop-off point in front of The Ritz-Carlton. The building was all red brick. It looked like an industrial plant that had been renovated.

Wang closed the car door, and walked inside past the gray-suited doorman, who held the door open for him. He walked quickly through the large red brick walled reception area and found the elevators, with only a passing glance to the reception desk. And then he was in the elevator. He'd spotted a security guard, but the man had shown no interest in him.

On the third floor, the corridor was wide and had a pale carpet and classy prints on the walls. A discreet security camera made it easy to understand why the guard was so relaxed.

If he tried to force a door open, they would know immediately. They probably had a staff member staring at him on a screen right now. He went straight to room 342 and rapped on the door. He smiled at the eye level brass peephole.

Nothing happened. Had she gone?

He rapped again, harder.

A click sounded. The door opened, but only the width of a finger.

34

Rob cleared his throat. "It's about Jackie," he said.

"Sure," said Faith. "Get here as quick as you can. I'm in room B3."

A black Chevy was waiting for him across the street from the complex. Twenty minutes later he was at TOTALVACS. When he reached room B3, it was empty. A closed laptop lay on the meeting room desk in the middle of the room.

He sat on one of the steel and black leather meeting room chairs and waited. The door opened a minute later.

"We don't have much time, Rob. I just asked Bishop to give us five minutes. He's champing at the bit." She stood near him, then pulled out the chair beside him and sat.

"What happened about Jackie?" Her tone had softened, but it still felt as if she was following some State Department guide to building empathy and getting information.

He suddenly regretted that he'd asked to speak to her about Jackie. She wasn't going to be sympathetic. What had he been thinking?

"Is this to do with Vladimir and your meeting?" said Faith. "A report I saw said he showed you his phone screen. What was on it, a picture of Jackie?"

140

He thought about denying it for a few seconds, but decided against it. "No, a video. And she looked alive." He shifted in his seat, sitting up straighter. "Are you watching me all the time?"

"Not when you're in the shower. I have my limits." She smiled. "What was going on in the video he showed you?"

"Jackie was trying to speak to me. She's alive. She has to be." Rob leaned forward. His stomach had tightened talking about it. "She had on a t-shirt she bought a few days before she supposedly died in London. She spoke about her medicine." He paused to breathe in. "She's not dead."

Faith put her hand up, as if to stop him saying any more.

"Wait, stop Rob, this is the type of psychological operation the Russians are really good at. They make you think someone close to you is dead or that the dead are alive and then tell you what to do to make it real. I know all about this garbage." She reached forward, put her hand on top of his, squeezed it, then let it go. Again, it seemed as if she was following some empathy guide.

"The Russians will use whatever dirty tricks they can to get you to do their bidding. You clearly haven't taken to honey traps, so psychological operations, psy-ops, is their next step. Did they ask you to interfere in the vaccine production process?"

He looked at her.

"I want to talk about this. I suggest we use my idea for a new version of the vaccine to fool the Russians into thinking they've won, and we keep going with the production of the first version."

"I'm glad you've come to your senses. And," she touched his hand again, "I'm sure Jackie would be proud of you."

She stood and headed for the door. She turned as she reached it and smiled at him. "I'm so glad you didn't make this more difficult," she said. "Come on."

He followed her to a large meeting room. Bishop was there. He didn't get up when they came in.

"I hope you've given up your crazy attempt to stop our manufacturing process, Dr. McNeil," was Bishop's greeting to Rob.

"That's why I'm here," said Rob. "I have a suggestion. You help us develop a second vaccine, which doesn't require refrigeration, and we proceed with the first now, for developed countries."

Bishop laughed. His whole body shook. "You sure have some cojones," he said. "Waltzing in here and issuing orders for what we should do." He pointed at Rob. "You know you're pushing your luck."

"The Russians want to stop our vaccine because they want to get theirs out first," said Rob. "This move will distract them. I expect they will try others."

"Rob was shown a video of his dead wife, to trick him into helping them," said Faith. "They claim she's alive. He told me about it a few minutes ago."

Bishop let out a humming noise. "You've been through the ringer, McNeil, and I appreciate you coming clean about what the Ruskies are up to." He lowered his voice. "Your work with us, on both stages of your vaccine, that's what's important. That's what Jackie would have wanted. To see your vaccine produced and saving lives, right?"

Silence filled the room. Rob could hear Bishop breathing. Bishop looked at his watch.

"Some of our production managers are expecting you in fifteen minutes for a video conference process and protocols meeting. I suggest you find some coffee. These meetings can go on for hours." Bishop stood. "I'm glad you're with us, McNeil," he said. "Believe me, if the Ruskies really did have a video of your wife alive, they'd torment you with it forever and a day."

He exited the room.

Rob turned to Faith. His lips were pursed. "Did he just say there's a chance the video is real?"

Faith shook her head. "No, he didn't. Don't believe any of it. Don't chase rainbows, Rob."

They got coffee and headed to a large meeting room where two production managers in white coats sat at the far end of the table and a big screen showed six others, some at their homes, some in offices.

Faith left him there. "When you're finished, call me," she said.

The meeting started with a request from one of the men in the room for Rob to describe the vaccine he had invented in detail. That took almost thirty minutes.

Then the questions started. That took four hours. Most of the people on the call were taking notes and he noticed the word RECORDING in red at a corner of the screen, which showed him when anyone was talking.

They now had a pretty complete set of instructions for the manufacture of his vaccine.

35

Wang pushed the door open. Gong Dao was wrapped in a big white towel.

"Why are you here?" she said, her tone frosty.

"I'm investigating you," he said.

"Go to hell, investigate yourself first," said Gong Dao, throwing a hand in the air. The towel slipped a little from one side, showing a tantalizing swathe of downy skin.

She turned and went into the main part of the large room. As Wang followed, he saw the room was a suite, with a separate bedroom to the left and a large reception room in front of him with couches, and a large screen TV, tuned to CNN, with the sound down.

Cushions from the couches were strewn around the floor, as if there'd been a fight going on in the room. Gong Dao turned, her hands wrapped tightly around her body, keeping the towel in place.

"And yes, you are totally right, as always, before you tell me. I'm the Chinese honey pot that important men crave. What are you going to do about it, Wang? I can report you today for interfering with an ongoing operation. Say your little piece and leave." She tightened her towel.

"What did you find out from Senator Harmforth?" said Wang. His tone was aggressive too. She wasn't going to bully him.

Gong Dao smiled, broadly. "I cannot tell you any operational details, you know that."

"Senator Harmforth is part of my operation too, Gong. I need you to cooperate." He took a step toward her. "Do not be mistaken. I am a senior manager in the Ministry of State Security now. You must cooperate with my instructions."

Her lip curled. "Your mission is not important. I know you want this senator to endorse changes at the WHO. And I know all about the cooperation you are looking for from him." She sat up straighter. "What I am part of is far more important." Her finger jabbed at him.

She tightened her towel, then swung it open, adjusting it, exposing her naked body for a long second. Wang's mouth opened as he stared.

She closed the towel. "Leave," she said, her nose high in the air. "I know what you want. But you have no chance. You are not man enough for me." She sneered. "You never were, and you never will be. Get out of here." She turned, went through the open door into the bedroom, and slammed it closed. The click of the key turning in the lock echoed in the air.

Unable to resist his anger and desire, he walked to the bedroom door, raised a fist as if he'd pound it, but held his fist in the air, shaking, instead. Then he turned and exited the suite. He'd get his revenge. He'd find a way. She'd made an enemy today.

On his way back to the embassy, he decided what he'd tell the head of security. He'd say that Gong Dao had offered herself to him and that he'd refused.

She would certainly report that he had come to her room. It would be his story against hers.

145

Laurence O'Bryan

He would report the conversation in detail, especially about Gong Dao's refusal to tell him what had happened with the senator. That was a definite warning flag, which they could not ignore. And neither could his bosses in the ministry.

She had to pay for all this.

Perhaps if she was transferred to some hellhole in the outer provinces, that might soften her up. He licked his lips. She definitely needed softening up.

36

Vladimir examined the mural on the wall. It showed a girl holding out bread and salt in front of her. A hand slapped onto his shoulder.

"It is good you could make it to our little celebration lunch," said the bald man. He had a long white scar below his left eye.

Vladimir slapped the man's shoulder in return. "You must know I don't usually get invited to such refined events, Ivan," he said, looking around the reception room in the Russian Embassy.

Ivan stepped back. "You do remember how I got this?" He pointed at his scar.

"Protecting the motherland from foreign agitators with my help," said Vladimir.

"Exactly, so I couldn't leave you out of this when I heard you were here. Come, join us." He pulled Vladimir by the shoulder toward a group of men standing at the head of a long, highly polished table, set with silverware and glittering goblets. A chandelier hung above.

"Welcome a true hero of Russia," said Ivan loudly as they approached. "No, no, not me; this man, Vladimir, is a true superhero. He destroys all enemies."

Vladimir looked at Ivan. His face was flushed, his smile a little too wide. The man was clearly nearing the end

147

of his tour of duty. He'd seen it before: the dropping of the guard and the loose talk at the thoughts of the dacha, the end of responsibilities and always wondering what mistake you had made, and the ever-present mistress finally by your side.

He looked at the faces around him. All of them at least looked like military men, so there'd be no fear in Ivan's mind that he was going too far.

But he was.

One of the group, a younger man, spoke. "I did not see you on the list of transfers from Moscow, comrade Vladimir." His smile lasted less than a second.

"A simple mistake, I am sure," said Vladimir. Already he was regretting accepting the invitation, but it had said his appearance was required, which meant only a real illness, which required a doctor, would be a good enough excuse not to appear.

Ivan slapped him on the back, hard. "This man is the reason we will soon take our rightful place leading the civilized world again. Let's drown one for him."

The men all raised their glasses, downed whatever was in them.

Ivan leaned toward Vladimir. "How goes the mission?" he said, his eyes bright.

"A success already," said Vladimir.

"Good, good, let us enjoy our lunch. The Borscht here is nearly as good as they make it in Minsk."

They sat around the table. The man beside Vladimir introduced himself as the military attaché to Washington. He launched into a vivid description of his time flying helicopters over Kabul. His efforts to impress Vladimir were transparent. Vladimir, as soon as he could, turned to the man on the other side.

That man glared at him.

"This is the Belarus room," said the man. "Did you know the Americans are trying to destabilize Belarus right now?"

"They try every crazy trick they can to diminish us. But I am one hundred percent sure we will be victorious with our great leader in charge of things," said Vladimir, spouting the expected reply.

The man slammed his fist on the table. "Yes, yes, and what is needed as a suitable reply to the Central Mis-Intelligence Agency is more riots here in the United States. Anything that sows chaos must be welcomed."

"It will happen," said Vladimir. "There are real grievances. That's what gets big crowds out."

The man's eyes opened wide. "Exactly. Big crowds can bring big changes. The stability that a country needs only comes about after a period of big changes. I look forward to it."

The man pushed his purple lower lip forward, glanced around. "I'm glad to see you don't use Telegram, that stupid message app these young men use to message their whores as soon as they reach the United States and can get to use it openly."

"There are still whores in Washington?" said Vladimir.

"The best Washington ones advertise on Russian-based websites now. Can you believe that?"

Vladimir excused himself and found the restroom. As he was washing his hands, Ivan came in.

"You'll be leaving after the Borscht, I expect," said Ivan.

Vladimir didn't reply. He continued drying his hands with a paper towel.

"What do you want me to do?" he asked.

Ivan checked the stalls were empty, then reached inside his jacket and pulled out an inch-long black pellet. It was one of the toughened ones you could swallow and expect to see, still shining, come out the other end in around thirty-six hours.

"Who?" said Vladimir.

"Wait for a message."

"I suppose you have records showing me as a psychotic loner and a traitor ready for any investigation, if I fail."

Ivan shrugged. "Of course. These things are ready for all of us, if we fail," he said. He washed his hands with great care.

"And anyhow, it's mostly true in your case, isn't it? Stints in the SVR and the FSB with all the people you've rubbed up the wrong way cursing at you behind your back."

"I speak my mind, Ivan. The Russian way. Our way. And I get the job done. That's why I'm here, isn't it?"

Vladimir strode from the restroom, went back to the reception room, and enjoyed the Borscht, slowly. Ivan had been right. It was the best this side of Minsk.

37

Rob woke early. He was on the internet by five. There would be no jog for him this morning. He'd arranged to be picked up at seven and taken to the TOTALVACS building. The breakfast there was great, so Faith had claimed. Tasty bacon, organic eggs, and hot pancakes with the best maple syrup in the world was her description.

She'd promised to be at the apartment building at seven-thirty to collect him.

At seven he sent a message to the number the Chinese had contacted him from. "Manufacturing stopped on my vaccine. Do you want me to help get yours moving?"

It was a risky message. Bishop would probably see it, but he didn't care. He might be able to extract some information about this Gong Dao from the Chinese. And he was only sewing fake news. And if they told him he was lying, he'd know TOTALVACS had a leak.

If anything, he was helping TOTALVACS. As seven-thirty came and went, he was picked up and driven into the city, in light traffic. He expected a call from Vladimir at any moment. But it didn't come, even though he kept his phone in his hand the whole way.

It was a calculated gamble. If Jackie was still alive, the Russians would figure out they had to do more to convince him. That was what he needed. He needed to talk to her. Properly.

At eight he was in the restaurant at TOTALVACS. There were only a few other people thinly spread out in the giant room. The hot food counter was closed. All that was available were individually packaged cereals, a selection of juices, and dishwater water from coffee machines. Faith must have been thinking about the breakfasts long before the virus.

No one was wearing a mask either, but people were keeping their distance and using the bottles of hand sanitizer on the walls. One thing was sure, hand hygiene had taken a great big leap forward with the virus.

At 8:05, Faith came in. She did not look happy.

"What are you doing texting the Chinese?" she said.

"I am helping TOTALVACS to find out if they have any Chinese spies," he replied, firmly.

"Yeah, yeah, right, and what are you going to give them?"

"Good morning to you too," he said.

"You know they want to revoke your security clearance," she said.

"I don't care," he said. He'd made a promise to himself on the way here, that he wasn't going to be the lab rat they wanted him to be. He had to focus on one thing now—Jackie—and if was she still alive, how could he free her?

He took a sip of his coffee. "You guys aren't reliable anyway."

"What?" she grimaced, anger flashing across her face.

"There's no hot breakfast. You said there would be."

She shrugged. "You're getting into bed with mass murders, Rob. You know they revere one of the biggest mass murders of all time, Mao. He has the blood of fifty million Chinese on his hands."

"They're not alone in revering dictators, Faith. Stalin had the same number of dead Russians on his conscience, and a lot of people in Russia would love to put him back in charge."

"There's no good excuse for helping the Chinese."

Rob shook his head. "Revoke my clearance. I don't care. Your people are super clever. I've given them enough information to finish the vaccine, both versions. They'll probably do it faster than I could too."

"You want to be a spy now." She sat opposite him. "I've been trying to help you, Rob." She looked serious. "I told them you were probably trying to find out about Gong Dao, because if your wife had been murdered, she'd be the person to ask about it."

"So, you can join dots," said Rob.

"You make it too easy."

"That's the plan."

Faith put her hands together as if she was going to meditate, or about to say something she didn't want to. "We can provide better information than your Chinese contact."

"Go on," he said. The conversation was getting interesting.

"There was a break-in at your house the day after we met, before we went to Beijing."

"What the hell?" He felt a feeling of violation, as if his most personal possessions had been strewn on the road.

"It was the Russians," said Faith.

38

Wang closed the door gently. The Head of Security at the Chinese Embassy waited for him behind a small wooden desk in an office crammed with locked filing cabinets and metal boxes. Three thin faded-red Chinese Ministry of Foreign affairs folders lay on his desk, near a set of yellow pencils in a row in front of an old Chinese calligraphy brush set with a long marble holder.

"You have been busy, Mr. Wang Hu," said the Head of Security.

"I am sure you are aware of the top-secret nature of my mission here," said Wang. He didn't sit on the wooden, straight-backed chair nearby. He hadn't been invited to.

"A senior embassy staff member of high rank, a Ms. Gong Dao, has complained formally, about you, Mr. Wang Hu."

Wang stared at a spot on the wall above the man's head.

"I understand you are from the old school of learning on the job, Wang Hu, but you are also expected to conform to all the latest directives, especially those from our great leader concerning the respectful treatment of women."

"I am aware," said Wang, stiffly. "And I have not committed any breach of the great leader's directives. Not even one." There was no choice in these situations but to

154

deny everything, unless confronted with multiple high-ranking witnesses.

To accept you had broken a directive would lead to instant dismissal and a return to Beijing under a cloud of shame on the next suitable flight, possibly with two guards or maybe more, depending on the infraction.

"Well, I expect she will have to withdraw the accusation, if she provides no evidence and no witnesses, but I must warn you, Wang Hu." He'd dropped the Mr. "I do not want to hear another accusation from her with your name involved in it." The Head of Security entwined his fingers and rested his elbows on his desk. He bent his head to one side.

"I understand affairs of the heart, young man, but you must put your head above everything. Not this." He pointed at his crotch.

"And finally, let me say, in case you have orders which may require you to move like the nine-tailed fox." He paused. His eyes were as hard as marbles. "Break no laws of the United States, while you are here in their land." His eyes narrowed. "There will be harsh repercussions if I have to mention your name to the ambassador. My order to this effect overrules any orders you have received in Beijing. Do you understand?"

"Yes."

"Dismissed."

Wang exited the office and closed the door. He would have loved to slam it, but to get away with just a warning after almost forcing his way into Gong Dao's room was a piece of good fortune, and he had to take it. One piece of good luck often led to another.

He went to the staff tearoom at the back of the embassy. It was as clear as mountain spring water what he had to do next.

39

Vladimir looked at the video playing on his phone. One thing was for sure, McNeil's wife, this Jackie lady, was a fine-looking woman. He could see how McNeil would find it difficult to give her up.

The woman on the screen held up an iPad type device with a picture of President Trump speaking outside the church near the White House, which he had walked to a few days before.

This would prove to McNeil that his wife was still alive. He'd failed to turn up that morning at the park for his run, so Vladimir had recommended that a new video be made with McNeil's wife. The man had to be taught a lesson.

At the end of the video, the woman handed the iPad device to someone. She looked frightened now. Her eyes were wide. She was handed a black hood. As she put it on, she shook.

This should be enough to get McNeil to do what was needed. He headed out of the embassy and climbed into the yellow cab waiting for him at the side exit. The taxi dropped him near McNeil's condo complex. He'd already received a message from the camera monitoring unit that a car had been tracked from TOTALVACS to this complex in the last half hour.

He would show the video to Rob. And this was not like the other video, which could easily have been a piece of video trickery. But he had to be careful. There could be no repercussions for Moscow. It was one thing knowing that a person believed to be dead was alive. It was something very different to share a video of that person being threatened. Deniability was the glue that kept many field operations alive. Flagrant deniability was only possible if a video disproving your case had not been watched a million times on YouTube.

He used a forged entry card at the unoccupied reception area for the condos and walked straight in and toward Rob's rooms. He hoped McNeil hadn't just eaten. The sight of your loved one being threatened had the power to turn people's stomachs. He'd had vomit on his shoes a few times, and once on his jacket too. He had been glad, a few times, that he only ever wore out of date baggy gray suits.

He knocked on the door of Rob's room, waved at the spy hole. The door opened a minute later. Rob stood aside to let him in. His face was grim.

Sitting in one of the chairs was the State Department spy he'd brought back with Rob from China.

"It is Faith, yes?" said Vladimir, giving Faith a half salute.

"Yes, you remembered, now why don't you tell me why you're harassing this American citizen with your clearly fake video. It's a grotesque insult to the dead to do this. Have you no shame?"

Rob put a hand up.

"Vladimir, what do you want? Why are you here?" He was angry.

Vladimir threw his hands in the air, as if he was the one who should be angry.

"I hate to break up your private reunion," he said. "But I have important news for my friend Dr. McNeil regarding his wife." He pointed at Faith. "And you are the people who spend half your lives doctoring videos of a few dozen protestors in Russia, to show that thousands are protesting against our president. Would you like to see the evidence for that?"

"No, I wouldn't. Spit it out. Why are you here?" said Rob.

"Ask your friend to leave or be quiet," said Vladimir, softly, nodding toward Faith.

"No," said Faith. "I'm not going anywhere."

"Why do you want her to leave?" said Rob.

"Because every word that spouts from her mouth is a lie. She will make me crazy with her lies piled upon lies. I won't be responsible for my actions if she stays and barks out lies." His voice grew angrier with each word.

Rob turned to Faith. "Please, let me find out what he has to say."

Faith pressed her lips together, made a frustrated noise in her throat, and nodded briskly.

"I promise to be quiet," she said.

"Good," said Vladimir. "Perhaps you will learn what so many American women need to learn—to respect their men."

Faith's mouth opened.

"Cut that crap out," shouted Rob. "Be respectful. You can leave now if you're going to continue with that."

"OK, OK," said Vladimir.

"What I have for you cannot be easily dismissed, Dr. McNeil. Your friend will tell you we can take any face from

159

a stolen video, perhaps from any smartphone account, and place it on a character who then says or does something that we want said or done, but she is wrong. I have never seen something like this to be faked. It's impossible." He pulled his smartphone from his pocket and started tapping at the screen.

Rob looked at Faith. Her face was a picture of skepticism.

Vladimir turned the screen to Rob. Faith came up beside him. The two of them stared at the video of McNeil's wife. Faith's face grew pink, and her mouth twisted in disdain.

Rob's looked interested at first, then sad, as he saw his wife. Then a distasteful expression came over it, as if he'd swallowed something bad.

"How can you show me this?" he bellowed. "How dare you take my wife's videos and make this." He swung a fist up into the air. "Get out of here. That's disgusting that you would bring that here. Go!" He pointed at the door. "Now."

Vladimir turned the screen back to himself. "You didn't watch it all." He shook his head. "None are so blind as those who cannot see."

"If you bother Dr. McNeil with these videos again, a complaint will be made to your embassy and you will be asked to return home to Russia as quickly as possible," said Faith, as Vladimir walked out of the room.

40

Wang knocked on the door of the on-site embassy doctor. A female voice called for him to come in. The doctor had a lilting Mandarin accent. She was probably from Canton and spoke Cantonese growing up and her accent carried over to her Mandarin.

"You have special request, yes, Mr. Hu," said the doctor as a greeting. She was small and had a dimple on her chin.

"Yes, you should have received a message from Beijing," said Wang.

"I did. I will provide the medicine requested."

Wang looked around the room. White shelves filled every wall. Each was stacked with medicines in a bewildering array of plastic containers of different sizes. One shelf held glass jars. Another had a row of herbs in envelope-shaped plastic bags.

"You have every medicine here," said Wang.

"Do you need something else?" said the doctor. "Perhaps a little boost?" She made a fist of her hand and raised it.

"No, no problems there." He wanted to ask for something to reduce desire, not raise it, but he couldn't. Every request would undoubtedly be logged into the computer system sitting on her desk and be visible to his superiors the next day.

In any case, the cure for what troubled him would be found in either winning Gong Dao or crushing her for the insults she had inflicted and the torture of unrequited desire she had put him through.

He put his hand out.

"I have been asked to do a check-up on you while you are here, Mr. Wang Hu, so please jump on the examination table." She pointed at the leather-covered table.

"I don't need this," said Wang.

"Just your blood pressure, temperature, and afterward a urine sample," said the doctor. She handed him a small plastic container.

"Every morning when I come to the embassy, someone takes my temperature," he said.

"Good, this is a second check," said the doctor, holding a thermometer gun to his forehead. "Now please, roll up your left sleeve."

As he was leaving the doctor's office, the doctor put her head to one side. "Do be careful with that medicine, Mr. Hu. It will reduce blood pressure very, very fast. Do not use it unless you are experiencing super high readings."

Wang nodded and left the room. Every morning when he came to the embassy, someone would have an opinion they wanted to share with him. Perhaps working here in America was as dangerous as he'd heard. The contagion of free speech and expressed opinions was hard to put an end to once anyone got into the habit.

It would be better when he got back to Beijing. People still had opinions there, but they knew their place and to keep their thoughts to themselves.

His next stop was the surveillance room. The senior officer was at a desk at the top of the room. Rows of operatives sat in front of him with their laptops on. There were forty-eight surveillance officers in the large, open-plan room. At any one time, they could be tracking the locations and cell phone data for thousands of individuals, both Chinese and those with an interest in China.

The room's walls were lined with a metal mesh, to create a Faraday cage, inside the larger Faraday cage of the embassy. This helped to ensure that any eavesdropping equipment that had been snuck into the embassy would not be able to pick up electronic signals from this room.

Wang went to the top of the room and saluted the senior officer. He was a lifetime staff member of the Ministry of State Security. He did what was expected of him without question.

The man watched Wang approach and returned his salute.

"Your target data will appear on your Baidu maps app on your phone as your next destination, Mr. Wang," said the officer. He kept his expression stiff.

"If the target has not moved in the previous two-hour window, the location will turn red. All data will be scrubbed from our records, on your request or the termination of your mission."

"All data will be copied to Beijing?" said Wang.

"Yes, we have that enabled."

"Good."

The eyes of half the room followed him as he exited. The women in the room, mostly young, would rarely see someone from Beijing down here in the bowels of the embassy. The makeup he used to hide his facial discoloration worked well, but some young people would wonder at the obvious slickness on his skin.

He remembered how Gong Dao used to prefer him without the makeup when he came to see her. She was attracted to him because of it, she'd said. Had it all been a lie? Had she just used him to get to the next more important man?

Well, soon she would face her just punishment for her lies and tricks. He would expose her for what she was. Her involvement with McNeil had given him the opportunity to do so, and he would not let it go now.

He went back to the tearoom and opened his Baidu map app. The next location was still red and she was at the hotel he'd left her in. It looked as if she'd taken the whole day off. Someone high up in the embassy clearly protected her.

41

Vladimir walked into Ivan's office on the third floor of the Russian Embassy early the following morning. Ivan was on the phone. It was one of those thin Russian office phones that had been popular in Moscow offices twenty years ago.

Vladimir sat, took out a Russian cigarette from the black cigarette box with the Russian eagle embossed on it lying on the desk. He picked up the black marble lighter and lit the cigarette. There was no ashtray. He tapped his ash in a plastic bin with a black eagle on it. He took it from beside a coffee table and two leather couches in the far corner of the room. The couches were stained. It looked like Ivan held parties here.

"No smoking in the offices anymore," said Ivan, coming up behind him. "Come here, I've found a way to get one of these windows open." He walked to a window and pushed at its handle. The window swung open and a cool breeze flowed in.

"Why do you have cigarettes and a lighter on your desk if we are not allowed to smoke in these offices?" asked Vladimir.

"The colleague I replaced shot himself here." Ivan pointed at the roof of his mouth. "When he received his late-stage cancer diagnosis after returning from Moscow. I

165

thought it would honor his memory if I left the room the way he had it for over twenty years."

"The things that went on back then," said Vladimir. "No one would believe it if we told them."

Ivan dropped his part-finished cigarette in a large coffee cup, a quarter full of cold coffee. Vladimir did the same with his.

"They would not believe it if I told them what you are up to now," said Ivan.

"It would be a lot easier, a lot less messy, Ivan, if Moscow supported me properly."

Ivan went back to his desk, sat down heavily, and said, "There is a lot going on, Vladimir. What you're doing is just part of a bigger operation. You will get the support you need, when it can be delivered."

"I know about the other parts, Ivan," said Vladimir, coolly. "I know we are tracking infected Russians and guiding them."

"Good." Ivan's expression gave little away.

"And I understand the objective of all this is above my paygrade, Ivan. I just want to get my job done and go home."

"What else do you need, Vladimir?"

Ivan's phone rang before Vladimir could answer. He picked up the handset, shouted, "Call me back in two minutes," and put the phone back in its cradle.

"I need a better video. The ones I have been sent are not working. That's it."

Ivan's face lit up. "What about this," he said. "Why don't I ask them to set up a live call from Dr. McNeil to his very alive wife."

"That would be a useful next step," said Vladimir.

"The boys back in Moscow are cagey about live calls. The Brits have a way to track calls through the internet cable entering Russia through Sweden and Finland, but we can figure something out."

"I have her medicine too," said Vladimir.

"That should seal it."

"Can you get it set up for tomorrow? Early morning here. Afternoon in Europe."

Ivan waved his hand through the air. "Miracles like speaking to the dead are easy for me to arrange. Getting it done on time is up to Moscow."

"You have good connections, Ivan."

"Do you think McNeil will want to meet her too?"

"I am sure he will; wouldn't any good husband? I will keep him waiting for that. It's the big pay-off. He'll have to follow orders like a good soldier before that," said Vladimir.

"Did the boys in Moscow think all of this through when they started the operation?" asked Ivan.

"I wasn't in on it at the start," said Vladimir.

"I have to admit it's a clever plan," said Ivan. Vladimir headed for the door. One thing was clear, Ivan knew a lot more than he was saying.

42

Rob walked into the restaurant at TOTALVACS, poured himself some coffee, and sat down. Faith arrived a minute later and joined him.

"They're talking about making face masks mandatory at all meetings," she said.

"I agree with it," said Rob.

"Maybe, but we're getting a lot of push back. Some people are saying we're overreacting. If the president isn't for it, we shouldn't be doing it."

"Any news on Gong Dao?" He had to keep himself busy while he waited for Vladimir's next move.

Faith shook her head. "When I told you she was in Washington, that didn't mean I'd track her movements for you."

"I didn't ask for that." He put a hand flat on the table. It was trembling. "This stuff with Vladimir is making me crazy, Faith. I barely slept last night. Look at my hand." He gripped his two hands together, closed his eyes for a long moment. "I need to know I've done everything I can for Jackie."

Her expression was unmoving.

"You're not a government drone," he said. "I got you out of China. You might still be there if I hadn't

168

demanded they release you. You owe me." His voice rose as he spoke.

"I don't owe you," said Faith, shaking her head. "But if I do tell you where she is, when we find her, it will be a one-off and you must not give away how you found her."

Rob smiled for the first time that day. "What happened to you?" he said. "That was easy."

Faith stood. "Bishop wants to see us."

She led the way to the elevator. They went down to the sub-basement. Level-3.

Faith led the way to a large room with a panel of computer screens on one wall. Two operators, with headphones on, sat at desks in front of the screens. The screens showed images of the front and sides of this building on K Street and the building at Fort Detrick. It also showed the restaurant and the interior of meeting rooms and labs. Text labels at the bottom of each screen indicated what was being observed.

One row of screens showed hotel entrances and streets around the TOTALVACS building.

Bishop was sitting at a table in an open area in front of the screens. He motioned for Rob and Faith to join him. They sat sideways to the screens. The chairs allowed them to rotate.

"We know you're being watched, Dr. McNeil. That's how your friend Vladimir found you. The Ruskies are a clever bunch, but you know that already." He looked downcast. "I'm real sorry they've resorted to such underhand tactics with you."

Rob waved his hand, dismissing Bishop's sympathies. "I understand you can help me find Gong Dao, the woman who visited my wife," said Rob.

Bishop shot a glance at Faith.

"My colleague discussed your request with me. There is a way we can assist you."

"How's that?" asked Rob.

"Let me make it clear, first, that you are not obliged to do anything you don't agree with for TOTALVACS or the United States government. We're not China. We don't compel compliance."

"What is it you want?"

"This person you want to contact, this Gong Dao, is on our radar. We'd like you to take her a message."

Rob looked skeptical. "A message? Are you crazy?"

"We want her to come over. It'll be your best shot at getting her to talk."

"You want her to defect?"

Bishop nodded.

"What makes you think she'll listen?"

"First, she's the right profile for monitoring. And second"—he smiled—"you're the right profile for the type of person she'll believe. You're not a trained spy. You're a scientist, someone who has suffered, as she has. You won't be recruiting her, OK, we have trained agents for that, but you'll plant the seed, you'll tell her we want her, and that she can have a new life as a millionaire in any city in the world. I believe Rio is nice this time of year."

"What the hell?" said Rob, angrily. "I don't want to manipulate her for you. Maybe she won't go for it."

Bishop looked like a dog whose bone was in reach.

"Rob, this is the best way to get her to tell us things," said Faith. "If you just ask her why she went to visit your wife, she can deny everything. This is our best shot."

The room went quiet as Rob thought about what he was being asked to do. "You think this will work?"

Bishop raised his hand. "Yes, if she comes over to our side, she's going to spill the beans on everything related to your wife: who ordered her to go there, was it official or some rogue operation, and anything else she can tell us. Our chance of getting reliable information jumps a thousand percent this way." He smiled.

The room went quiet again.

"So, where is Gong Dao?"

"She's on her way to New York. As we speak, she's being driven down I-95. We expect her to reach Manhattan in about two hours."

"You know where she's going?" said Rob.

Bishop looked at Faith. It was a searching look.

"We have a hunch. We're good at that."

Rob looked around the room, looked up at the camera pod. "Is TOTALVACS some part of Homeland Security? You guys are good with your surveillance," he said.

"Any large corporation needs good security," said Bishop. "But to answer your question, no, we're not part of Homeland Security, although we do align ourselves with their mission."

"Recruiting Chinese defectors is their mission?"

"Rob, this is about killing two birds with one stone," said Faith. "We all get to find out if China's been seeding the virus, as you've been claiming they did with your wife, and if she admits to it, we'll find out how, and lots more details. It'll help TOTALVACS and Homeland Security and other federal agencies understand what we're up against here in the United States and hopefully how we can stop it all."

"I don't want what happened to Jackie to get lost if Gong Dao does come over," said Rob. "I need to know what they did will go public, if she admits it."

Bishop shook his head, as if shaking off water. "I gotta tell you, I don't have time for debate on that. If you don't want to cooperate, so be it. We'll do it ourselves. Expecting us to go public is unrealistic. There's so much going on these days the story of one infection will be buried in five minutes. If the Chinese think you have found some way to expose them, expect them to start leaking your internet search history for the past ten years, and your wife's—with added child porn. They're good at smearing people. Is that what you want people to know about you?"

Rob sighed, put his hands up. "OK, we do it your way. When do we get going?"

Faith smiled. "There's a car waiting. We can use a blue light and cut an hour off the journey."

"You're coming?"

"Yeah."

"You better go," said Bishop. "There's a protest feeder march passing across K Street soon."

"The BLM crowd don't want to give up," said Rob.

"It's the out of towners I worry about," said Bishop. "Thugs bussed in to break windows and throw rocks. We see a lot of people who are not DC people when we look at security camera feeds."

"You can identify people on the street?" said Rob.

"Sure, with facial recognition. We watch for troublemakers."

"And then stop them?"

Bishop shrugged. "If we need to."

43

Wang looked out the window of the embassy Mercedes as they sped down I-95. Gently rolling hills with a thick canopy of trees lay in all directions. You could imagine what this land must have been like before the Europeans arrived, the native tribes living close to nature, oblivious to what was coming.

He'd read a lot about how the United States had grown to its position at the top of the world in the twentieth century. What was obvious from the attempt to make America great again, was that its position had slipped from unassailable, to ripe for overthrow.

China was on track to be the world's leading nation within decades. All others would learn then what it meant to kowtow. He looked at his Baidu map app again.

She was an hour ahead of him.

He leaned forward to speak to the driver. "Can you go faster?"

The driver shook his head. "I must keep to the speed limit at all times," he said. "No matter what my passenger says." He looked ahead, not engaging with Wang's eyes boring into him from his rearview mirror.

An hour later Wang got his first glimpse of Manhattan, gray skyscrapers looming on the horizon as they came over a ridge. He opened the Baidu app, tapped at it. It looked like she'd stopped at the UN building on the East River. If Gong Dao went in there, he'd have to contact the embassy. But wasn't it closed? Perhaps better to wait nearby and see where she was heading.

"Head for 45th Street, near the East River," he told the driver.

The traffic was light crossing the George Washington Bridge into Manhattan and heading across town. He kept his Baidu app open. When they reached the end of 45th Street, he got out.

"Head back to Washington," he told the driver. I'll take it from here."

The map icon showed Gong Dao was now in the building opposite the United Nations. From what he could see from a search online, the building had a Hilton hotel in the top section of the skyscraper. That had to be where Gong Dao had gone. But why, and who was she meeting?

He walked to the entrance of the skyscraper at One United Nations Plaza. The building was a glass and steel monstrosity rising high into the deep blue afternoon sky. There were few passersby, most of them wearing face masks, as he was. When he went inside the building, he was stopped by security guards near the elevators.

"No visitors," said one of the guards, a giant black man.

"Is the hotel open?" asked Wang.

"Only for first responders, health care workers, and local staff," said the other guard, a barrel-chested redhead.

"I am staying with someone," said Wang. "They have a room booked."

"Room number and name," said the black guard.

Wang looked at his phone. "I'm waiting for a message with that. I'll come back," he said. He exited the building and walked slowly up the street as he called the hotel.

"Put me through to Gong Dao's room," he said when someone finally answered. There was a brief hesitation, then the voice said. "We have no one staying here by that name."

44

Rob sat up in the back of the Chevy. It had been a non-stop drive down I-95. He was ready for a break. Most of the way to New York, Faith had been tapping at her phone, answering emails it looked like.

He wasn't in the mood for small talk. It felt as if he'd been sandbagged. He was now an unofficial agent for the State Department and TOTALVACS security. They'd got what they wanted first, him training their vaccine team, and now they were going to use him to try to turn someone.

One thing was sure, he was going to expose what the Chinese had done, if he did get an admission from this Gong Dao in person. He didn't care if they locked him up. If the Chinese had deliberately infected his wife, maybe they'd done it to others too. How many had died because of this? It couldn't be hidden from the world. It had to come out.

Perhaps there could be something like the Nuremberg trials after the virus faded away. Getting justice for people who'd been deliberately infected was not a difficult concept. In some jurisdictions, you could be jailed for deliberately spreading HIV. Why should state actors get off the hook?

But first, there had to be credible witnesses, people who would spill the beans on the methods, purpose, and plans of all those involved in it. He had to get information from Gong Dao.

"Where are we going in Manhattan?" he asked.

"The United Nations."

Rob looked it up on his phone. "It says here it's closed."

"It is," said Faith.

"So where are we really going?"

"You'll see."

They drove through midtown and reached the United Nations Plaza at a little after four that afternoon. The streets had been almost empty, except for the occasional bus, taxi, and garbage disposal truck. Manhattan seemed wounded, its life blood drained, the crowds of people on the streets and the lines of honking cars all gone, and who knew when they'd return.

"Everything is closed around here," he said, as the Chevy pulled up by the sidewalk.

"Trust me," said Faith, as she opened the door. "Thanks for the drive," she called to the driver as they got out. He didn't reply.

"This way," she said. She headed into the glass and steel tower in front of them. When they got inside, they were stopped by security guards. Faith pulled out her State Department badge and they waved her and Rob through.

"Is Gong Dao staying here?" said Rob.

"Well done, Sherlock," said Faith. She entered one of the elevators marked for the Millenium Hotel.

There were virus warning signs in the elevator and, after it had risen to the twenty-eighth floor, where the hotel started, they were confronted with an empty lobby, a bank of hand sanitizing equipment and a smell of disinfectant.

"There's a suite booked," said Faith. "Someone will come with a room pass in the next few minutes. They know we've arrived." She nodded at the security camera pod high up on the wall.

"What room is Gong Dao in?" he said.

"Near us," she replied.

He sanitized his hands and read other notices pinned to the walls. The hotel offered breakfast bagels and fruit, delivered to your room, and discounted laundry services for first responders.

A staff member arrived and placed two key cards on the main reception desk, near a bottle of hand sanitizer. The woman was black, tall, and elegant. She looked harassed.

"I am sorry, we are totally understaffed today." She blinked. It looked as if she was going to cry.

"You've had it rough here in New York?" said Rob.

She nodded. "Yeah, please enjoy your stay. I'm sorry, I have to leave you. Your breakfast will be delivered to your room if you order it by midnight."

They headed back to the elevators.

"The two of us will stay in one suite?" said Rob, looking at the cards he'd picked up and cleaned with the sanitizer. He handed one to Faith.

"It's a two-bedroom suite. They all are on that floor," said Faith. "It's all they had left."

"How soon can I knock on Gong Dao's door?"

"She's not in the building now. We'll order room service and wait until she arrives before knocking on any door."

"She's definitely staying here?" said Rob.

"Yep, we have eyes on her."

"When will she be back in her room?"

"I don't know, Rob." Faith sounded irritated. "Whenever she finishes her business here, I guess."

"What business?"

Faith didn't reply.

45

Vladimir waited at one of the hot desks in the Russian Embassy. They were reserved for senior visitors from the motherland. There were six desks, separated by thick wooden screens. Only one other person was at a desk; a young man who looked to be on his first assignment.

Vladimir watched CNN on his phone, then RT, the Russian station for people who speak English. He wanted to see if the American TOTALVACS company had announced their partnership with McNeil's institute in Oxford yet. There was a possibility they were still negotiating the terms, but he had to assume that TOTALVACS would not be deterred by simple things like legal agreements. There was too much at stake.

He was surprised they hadn't announced the partnership already. Did that mean the marriage was not going as well as they'd hoped? He needed someone on the inside. McNeil had to be that person.

His phone buzzed briefly. He switched to his message app.

A video had dropped into his phone. It had arrived earlier than he expected. He looked around; no one was nearby. He started the video.

"Hello, Rob," said the woman on the screen.

She paused, nodded, then said. "Rob, I haven't much time, please listen." The woman looked around, as if she was being watched, then said angrily. "Wait, Rob, just listen."

Vladimir smiled. It was perfect. It assumed McNeil would be trying to get her to respond to him. They were genius with such messages back in Moscow. And there was no possibility of a trace this way, from State Department tech geniuses. The video could be stored on a server in New Jersey, and there'd be no doubt that the person they were watching was real.

What helped, of course, was when you actually had some real video.

Getting people to do what you wanted only required one thing. Leverage. Not much had really changed.

46

Rob rocked from side to side in the shower stall. Being in New York had brought back memories of the time he and Jackie had visited the city a few years ago. The video Vladimir had shown him went around in his head, in a mental loop. She looked almost the same as she'd looked in the video they'd made that weekend.

He closed his eyes and said a prayer to a God he didn't really believe in. *Please, make Jackie be alive, please.*

He knew though that it was a long shot, but it was one that couldn't be ignored. If she was alive, they'd have to convince him it was true. The only thing that would do that was if he and Jackie had a real conversation. And if she was alive, they would not give up because he didn't believe them.

They would keep coming back. Which meant they'd probably be contacting him soon.

He dried off, looked at himself in the mirror. Jackie would have wanted to cut his hair if she'd been with him. He rubbed his chin. He would let his stubble grow. There was a new toothbrush in its wrapper on a shelf. He had no idea who'd put it there, but he used it, then dressed and went into the main room of the suite. Faith wasn't there.

He turned on the news. Every TV channel was talking about death rates and telling harrowing stories about people who'd died. Everyone was trapped in a collective nightmare they couldn't wake up from. How stupid so many people had been, thinking the world could avoid a pandemic, just because we'd come so far with our medicine and our not-so-clever safeguards, which were only part implemented anyway.

And now death was all around.

He got an urge to email TOTALVACS and see how the production process was coming. He opened his email, blinked.

There was an email from Jackie, from her email address.

Rob,
I'll call you this evening.
Please, please do what they say.
Jackie.

His heart was beating fast. He groaned. Could this be real? Or was he being tortured? He almost threw the phone at the wall in frustration. But he didn't. He looked at the email again and replied instead.

Jackie,
I need to talk to you properly.
Call me.
Rob.

As he sent the email, Faith came out of her room. Her face looked pinched.

"We're supposed to go back to Washington," she said.

"What?" he said.

"There's something going on. I can't say any more."

Rob opened his phone and turned it to her.

"Wow," she said, after reading the email.

"I'm being tortured," he said. "Do none of you give a damn about what's happening to me? What am I supposed to do, ignore it all?" He raised his hands in front of him as if he was grappling with something.

Faith looked at her watch. "I want it all to stop it, Rob, and I'll do anything I can to stop this bullshit. But we're being picked up at eight, it's the soonest a driver can get here," she said. "The pandemic is messing it all up." She raised her hands. "We've been ordered out of here." She looked frustrated.

Rob looked at the time on his phone. "What can we do in three hours?"

Faith was silent, her lips pressed together, as if assessing something. Then she spoke. "We do what we were going to do—eat."

"What?"

She pointed at Rob's feet. "Put your shoes on," she said. She put a finger to her lips.

He put his shoes on and they left the room without saying any more. The door clicked behind them.

"What the hell, Faith? Are we being listened to?" said Rob.

"I assume every room that TOTALVACS books for me is bugged," said Faith. She started down the corridor.

"Where are we going?" said Rob. "To find Gong Dao?"

"Yes." She was walking fast. She passed the elevators and kept going.

Rob was at her shoulder. "What room is she in?"

They turned a corner. A service cart with a pile of towels on it stood to one side of the corridor. Beyond it, the corridor ended with the gray door of a service elevator. Faith pressed the button to summon the elevator. Nothing happened.

She walked back along the corridor to a room where the door was open. She knocked on the door.

A maid with her hair pulled back and wearing a face shield and mask appeared. She was carrying a bucket.

Faith flashed her badge. "Please open the service elevator," she said. "We need it."

The maid stared at her, then at the badge again, then went to the elevator. She used a key on a chain to get the button to work. Then she turned away and left them, as if afraid of standing near them for too long.

After they stepped inside, Faith pressed the basement button. "This is the best guess one of our staffers had for where Gong Dao was earlier," she said. "Her signal was in the same place, but getting weaker. Then it disappeared."

"She's in the basement?"

"We found out there's a connecting tunnel to a set of underground meeting rooms under the UN plaza. They're used when officials from one state want to meet other officials without being seen coming and going."

"Won't it all be closed up?"

"It should be, but countries who use it regularly can probably request access if they have a good reason."

"You think this Gong Dao has access?" he said. "And we're just going to walk in? I thought that the UN building was considered a separate territory, not part of the United States."

"Nope," said Faith. "Not true. They effectively waved all that separate territory stuff for our fire, police, and maintenance support, though we don't make it obvious."

She tapped the pocket in the black trouser suit where she kept her badge. "This will get us in anywhere."

The elevator stopped and the doors opened. Ahead was a wide corridor with room service trolleys in a line down one side. It was brightly lit, and the only noise was the hum of the fluorescent lighting. Another corridor led straight ahead.

"Either way looks right to me," said Faith. "What do you think?"

Rob closed his eyes and imagined where they would be if they were on the ground floor. "I reckon we go straight ahead. The passage should lead under the plaza."

They walked down the corridor until they reached a steel turnstile that filled the passage from top to bottom.

"This must be to block people the hotel doesn't want getting in," said Faith.

Rob pointed at a small metal plate on the wall beyond the turnstile. "I bet our room cards will let us back in too."

"We'll soon find out," said Faith. She pushed through the turnstile, then tapped the metal plate. The turnstile clicked and allowed her to push it, as if she wanted to go back into the hotel.

Rob went through and they walked on. The corridor beyond was not well lit. It disappeared into gloom.

A grinding noise could be heard now. Faith looked at him, her eyes wide.

"Have you heard about the slaughterhouses that used to be on this spot?" she asked.

"No." Rob looked at the walls. They weren't concrete here. They were thin red brick.

"Yeah, they're overrun with rats. The tenements that surrounded the slaughterhouses had a bad reputation. A lot of people used to get ill."

Parts of the brick walls were stained yellow and green. They kept going. Soon the walls were covered in concrete again. The grinding noise disappeared behind them too. They reached a T junction in the corridor and stopped.

"You think Gong Dao came this way?"

"Yes," said Faith. "You want to go back?"

Rob shook his head. "No way. We have to find this Gong Dao," he said.

"OK, let's keep going," said Faith. She looked down one corridor, then the other.

"It's all a bit James Bond, isn't it?" said Rob.

"Do you want me to show you the plans for their underground submarine pens?" said Faith.

Rob shook his head. He was thinking about the email he'd received. Was he wasting time on a wild goose chase? Was Jackie alive somewhere, waiting for him? Doubt gnawed at him.

"Don't believe that email," said Faith.

She must be a mind reader.

"Which way are we going?" said Rob.

"Your call. I'm doing this for you," said Faith.

Rob looked up at the curved roof, tried to figure out where they might be in relation to the street above. "Left," he said, confidently, though he didn't feel it.

They headed down a well-lit corridor until they reached a gray metal door. It was locked. As they were trying the handle, they heard voices behind them, in the distance. Then laughter.

47

Wang ended the call. The embassy had booked a room for him in a hotel in midtown, one of the few still taking guests. He'd also sent a message to Beijing. His assistant at the Ministry was tasked with finding out which room Gong Dao was staying in.

Now he had to wait until he was called back. He walked around the block. He would stand out like a dead dog if he hung around near her hotel.

Bitterness grew inside him, like a teacup filling to finally overflow, as he thought about how Gong Dao had used him, and how she might even now be in the arms of her lover, the senator, smiling at what she'd done to him. His teeth gritted. He had to separate his mission from his feelings. He had to be careful. Then an image of her smiling face came to him. A noise distracted him.

His phone was buzzing. A message had come in on his Ministry message app.

Return to Washington. Your driver will come for you. He will message you.

He turned his phone off and put it back in his pocket. He could be free. He could say he'd never seen the message. It would be a few hours before they even noticed. The summons had been abrupt, but what really got under his skin was that Gong Dao's mission was clearly more important than his.

What could be more important than bringing the WHO more closely under Chinese control?

He walked on. Perhaps he had enough time to get into her hotel. And she had flaunted herself to him. That could be a deliberate challenge to him. She was testing him, seeing if he would fight for her. And if she wasn't, could he let some stupid American take her? No, he couldn't.

He might risk everything, but he didn't care. He passed an all-American diner; it was shuttered, then a Lebanese restaurant, then a Chinese restaurant, also shuttered. A hand-written note on the door requested customers to order at a telephone number for local delivery. He could order to his hotel.

And that was when it came to him. The yellow dragons could help him. Their people who he'd met at the *Eye of the Ocean* in Beijing would be able to connect him with their people here in Manhattan.

He turned his phone on. A message from the driver had arrived.

Pick up in one hour.

There was another message with a number waiting for him too. The message was a number. His colleague in Beijing must have found out Gong Dao's room number.

He didn't have long before they'd be looking for him.

He pulled up the number the woman at the restaurant in Beijing had given him and called it. All he would ask for was a contact at a friendly Chinese restaurant that was still open in midtown. This way, even if his superiors in Beijing were listening to his calls, nothing untoward would go on.

He wanted a Chinese meal before going back to Washington. What could they say?

"I need to order some food," he said, when his call was answered.

"Where are you, Wang Hu?" said a young woman.

"Near United Nations Plaza in New York," he said.

There was a long silence, so long he wondered if the woman had gone. Then she replied.

"Please go to the *Eye of the Ocean* on 42nd Street. Rap three times on the door, then twice. The food there is glorious. Thank you for calling."

48

"This will stop him in his tracks," whispered Vladimir to himself, as he looked at the latest video to arrive from Moscow.

It showed Rob's wife, crying.

"That would stop an elephant."

He would tell Rob to be at the park in the morning and then give him the task. The risk of contamination was the key reason only a few people were allowed to visit a vaccine manufacturing facility. But Rob would be allowed anywhere at TOTALVACS.

And he could order a test of the vaccine product. Even the smallest detectable contamination would be sufficient to force TOTALVACS to start again.

All Vladimir's work would be vindicated then. Even if his mission was deniable, his masters in Moscow would know that he had succeeded in everything they'd asked, again. The Russian vaccine would be released first. Dozens of world leaders would order it from Russia. The West would be beaten in the great vaccine race.

He headed for the staff restaurant in the basement of the Russian Embassy. He didn't like mixing with embassy staff. There was always a chance he might bump into someone who knew him, someone who remembered him from some previous mission and could guess why he was

Laurence O'Bryan

here. But he'd looked at the telephone extension list of
Russian staff at the embassy—none of the names were
familiar. There were a few other Vladimirs on the list,
products of the popularity of their president twenty-five
years ago, and a few western first names, but no names he
recognized.

He sat on his own and ate a surprisingly good Beef
Stroganoff. As he was finishing, a young Russian woman
sat opposite him.

"You're lucky," she said. "The Beef Stroganoff will
be off the menu next week. Our beef supplies from the
motherland are nearly all gone and our chef will not use
American beef. No way." She made a dismissive noise.

He shrugged, looked away.

"Are you the agent from Moscow everyone is
talking about?"

He shook his head. "No. I am a plumber," he said.

She smiled at that. "Would you like to join us for
some real Moscow coffee?" She turned and pointed at a few
young people at the far end of the room. A young man
who'd been at the lunch the other day raised a paper cup to
him.

"Maybe I should have your boyfriend arrested for
telling you who I am," he said, giving her an icy stare.

"That one? He's not my boyfriend," she said. "And
I know exactly who you are, comrade Vladimir. I am this
embassy's counter-intelligence unit head." She pushed her
head forward, her eyes unsmiling. "We are getting younger,
yes? And that means you can talk to us without breaking
your mission protocols."

"And start by coming over for coffee?" he asked.

"Yes." She stood and headed for the group, who were all now staring at him.

49

Rob and Faith ran as quietly as they could back down the corridor. By the time they reached the turnstile, the laughter and voices were gone.

"They must have come the other way. Do you think it was her?" said Rob.

"Probably," said Faith. "Let's try to catch up to them."

She tapped a room card on the metal panel by the door. They pushed through and ran on to the elevator.

The door opened, but it took a long time.

"What floor?" said Rob.

"Ours." Faith pressed the button for the thirty-fifth floor.

"We could knock on her door," said Rob. "If that was her, she's probably just gone into her room. I bet it was her. The elevator takes a long time to get down from thirty-five."

Faith smiled. "You knock on her door. Tell her you want to find out about Jackie. She'll see there's no one with you. Tell her if she doesn't speak to you, you'll be going to CNN and telling them she's a Chinese spy who spread the virus in London."

"What if she doesn't answer?"

194

"Put this under the door." Faith held out a business card she'd pulled from her pocket.

It had the name Senator Harmforth on it, a United States Senate seal, and his cell number.

"How did you get this?" asked Rob.

"Long story. Just say you know who she's been meeting." Faith pointed down the corridor. "Suite 3562. If she knows we're onto her, it'll be easier to get her to come over. Just remember," Faith's voice lowered, "tell her we'll protect her. And tell her she's about to be called back to Beijing and purged. They all live in fear of ending up in a camp for something they didn't even know was against the rules. And in her case, she's definitely broken the rules."

Rob headed down the corridor. When he looked around, Faith was gone. He reached 3562 and listened. He heard nothing, not even the sound of a TV in some distant room. Did he really want to do this? Knocking on the hotel door of a Chinese agent to get her to defect was a big step.

He put his hand near the door, held it still.

He had to do this.

He rapped twice on the door. Nothing happened. He rapped again, even harder. He thought he heard a noise through the door. He couldn't be sure. He held up the senator's card to the peephole.

"I need to speak to Gong Dao," he said, loudly.

Nothing happened. He listened, turned away from the door. The sound of indistinct shouting filled the corridor. Someone had turned on a TV news channel. It must be showing a Black Lives Matter demonstration. He pushed the card Faith had given him under the door, then rapped on it again.

A door down the corridor opened and a doctor in a blue emergency room outfit came out of the room and went down the corridor, fast, glancing at him only once.

And the door he was knocking on opened. It was on the chain. A voice said, calmly, "What you want?" It was the voice of a young Chinese woman.

"I need to talk to you," said Rob. "My wife died in London a few weeks ago. Someone from your embassy there called on her before she died. I want to find out if the person sent to visit my wife was infected with the Coronavirus. I'm trying to find out why she died. Please, help me."

"Your name Dr. McNeil?" asked the voice.

"Yes."

"Your wife not dead," came the voice. "Now please, leave me alone."

50

The *Eye of the Ocean* restaurant on 42nd Street had a jet-black marble frontage, elaborate gold lettering, and gold double-sized main doors with giant red eyes embossed on them. The doors were closed. There was no notice in the window.

He rapped three times on the door, then twice. Nothing happened. He looked up at the skyscraper above the restaurant. United States flags ran in a row above the frontage. Had they not got the message?

He waited.

A taxi cruised by. The driver, a man with a cap and a blue face mask, stared at him.

The door of the restaurant opened. A young woman held it open two inches.

"Yes?" she said.

"I'm Wang Hu. I was told you could help me. I came from Beijing."

"We only serve few people now," said the young woman. "But you can come in." She bowed, opened the door for him.

After he went inside, she closed the door and led him up a wide wooden staircase with an elaborate gold handrail carved with dragons on each side.

At the top of the stairs, she turned right and pushed open the sliding door to a large room with a black marble-topped bar at the far end. Behind the bar were glittering bottles of alcohol of every type. White leather stools stood in the front of the bar. Tables, with chairs standing on top of them, filled the room. The wallpaper had yellow dragons on it.

"Please, wait here," said the woman.

He sat on one of the stools. A painting behind the bar showed a scene from an old Chinese restaurant, probably in Shanghai, with slim Chinese beauties in flapper dresses and hair bands, and men wearing fedora hats and baggy suits.

"You like our private bar?" came a voice. He turned. The woman was probably over seventy, but still beautiful, with her hair in a black bob, with one side lower than the other, like a knife. Her outfit was a plain black dress.

She bowed, stopped well away from him. The face mask she wore was pure white and had small filters at the side.

"It is not often we get a visit from the Ministry of State Security," she said.

"I'm sure you get plenty of Chinese state visitors," said Wang.

"A few. Not many. My name is Lian. What can we do for our esteemed friend?"

"Are you connected with the friends I met in Beijing in Ghost Street?"

She held her right hand up, raised her little finger the same way the woman in the restaurant on Ghost Street had done.

He nodded. "I am here on a personal matter, Lian. I need to gain access to the Millenium Hotel near the United Nations. A friend of mine is staying there. I want to surprise her. I need access to the hotel, that's all."

"Your friends at the ministry can't help with this?"

"I cannot ask their help for a personal matter."

Lian shook her head slowly from side to side. "This will not be easy," she said. "Do you know this woman?"

"We are old friends," said Wang.

Lian shook her head. "I cannot help a man who wishes to violate one of the flowers of the middle kingdom."

Wang raised his voice as he spoke. "There will be no violation."

"You swear to that?"

"Yes."

She bowed low. "Will you perform a simple task for us, when we ask you, Mr. Wang, if we help in this matter?"

Wang looked down at the polished wooden floorboards. He could feel that this was a moment where his life might change. His decision now could put him in their hands forever. Should he agree to her terms? His breath shuddered in his throat as a vision of one perfect night he'd spent with Gong Dao came to him. How could he say no?

He nodded.

"Please say it clearly for the camera," said Lian. She pointed at the glistening security camera in a corner of the ceiling, facing them.

"I will do as you wish in return."

"You must love this woman very much," she said.

He didn't reply. He was already regretting what he'd committed to. If only he hadn't gone to Gong Dao's hotel in Washington. If only she hadn't teased him, dismissed him, perhaps he'd still be there, doing the job he was supposed to be doing.

"Your promise will be tested," Lian said. "But we will not ruin you." She smiled. "We will even help you again in the future."

He turned, looked at the bar. "May I take a shot of that one?" he pointed at a bottle wrapped in old brown paper, with a golden string tied around the neck and a triangular golden label.

"Our best Guotai? You have good taste, Mr. Wang. Each of the seven times this one is distilled, they use golden sorghum as a filter." She went to the end of the bar, lifted a part of the counter, and went behind it. She took the Guotai bottle down, opened the string, took the stopper out of the bottle and poured a little into a wide-necked crystal glass. She passed the drink to him.

"Raise your glass to the success of this mission," she said. "I will be back soon."

Wang sipped, savoring the mellow taste of the Guotai.

51

Vladimir raised his vodka glass, looked at it. "This is good vodka," he said. Then he knocked the vodka back.

"The best," said Katerina, the embassy counter-intelligence unit head. She downed her shot, poured them both another. The rest of the group had disappeared, heading back to an apartment they shared.

Vladimir raised his glass to his lips, then put it down. "What is it you want from me?" he asked. His tone was wary now.

"Why should I want anything but you and your company?" said Katerina with an open smile.

Vladimir put back his head and laughed. Two people at a far table stopped eating and stared at him.

"Stop it," said Katerina. "You look like one of those old-timers who went mad after working at Laboratory X."

"How do you know I didn't work there?" He put the undrunk glass of vodka back on the table and pushed it away a little.

"OK, smart guy, there is something you can do for me," said Katerina.

Vladimir made a winding motion with his hand, as if to pull something out of her.

She leaned toward him. "I know you are on a top-secret mission," she said.

"I can't confirm or deny that," said Vladimir. His gaze held steady on her eyes.

"I heard you are tracking someone who came from the United Kingdom."

"I can't confirm or deny or deny that either."

She shook her head and her hair spun around. "Are you enjoying yourself?" she asked when she stopped.

"No," he replied, but he was smiling.

52

Rob put his foot in the crack between the door and doorframe. "I don't believe you," he said.

The door closed, then burst open. A young, slim, Chinese woman in a low cut cocktail dress was on the other side. She had her smartphone out and was filming him.

"Everything you say and do is going into the cloud. What is it you want?" Her tone was clipped.

Rob put his hands up as he passed her and let the door close behind him. When he was fully in the room, he turned to her.

"I'm not a danger to you," he said.

"You have two minutes. I'm expecting someone."

He backed into the center of the reception room. The suite layout was the same as his room.

"How do you know my wife isn't dead?" he asked. It was the best opening line he could think of.

"Someone told me about your big goose chase," she said. She stayed standing near the door.

"That's it?" Had he started this right?

"Yes, sorry. I can't help you any more." She reached for the door handle.

"Maybe I can help you," he said. Perhaps he should get straight to it.

"I don't need your help."

"I heard you were about to be called back to Beijing."

Gong Dao shrugged, but he noticed a slight flicker across her eyes, her eyelids fluttering.

"Please go, right now," she said. "I will scream if you don't. There are people I know in the suite opposite. They will come and rescue me. You will be arrested."

"There's no need to scream." Rob raised his hands. Had he blown it? "Just two more questions, please. Answer them and I will go." He paused. She stared at him.

"Did you visit my wife while I was in Paris?"

She shook her head, looked him in the eye. "This mission of yours is doomed," she said.

"Please answer the question."

She stared at him, then said, "Yes, I did visit your wife." She shrugged, as if it was unimportant what she'd just admitted to.

"Why?"

"To return an item you left behind on your previous trip to Wuhan. It was a simple call to your door. I did nothing wrong."

"She got sick soon after." He spoke slowly.

"I have answered your questions. What happened to your wife after my visit is not my responsibility. You will go now."

Rob took a deep breath, pointed at Gong Dao. "I will go, but first you should know, there is a purge starting in Beijing. Those who've broken rules will be going to re-education camps." He spoke slower now. "I've been told to offer you a way out."

Gong Dao shook her head. "I need no way out."

Rob's phone buzzed in his pocket. He took it out, turned it on. A picture of an older Chinese woman filled the screen. Chinese characters were overlaid on the image. Text was underneath. *Show her this.*

He held his phone out for Gong Dao to see the picture.

"You think pictures of my mother will make me betray my country," she shouted. "You are wrong. Get out!"

Rob's phone buzzed again. It was a text message this time.

53

Wang walked down the wide stairs of the restaurant. At the bottom stood a young Chinese man in a black suit. He looked like the ideal bank worker.

"Come, you can share my room at the Millenium," said the young man in American-accented Mandarin. Wang followed him through the main room of the restaurant, down a corridor, and through a fire door into an alley with garbage cans lined up on each side.

The young man didn't talk. He checked the fire exit was locked after Wang came through and then led the way down the alley. At the next street, he turned toward the East River. At a crossing, they waited for the pedestrian light to turn green. There was no traffic. The young man glanced at Wang.

"Are you really with the Ministry of State Security?" he said, softly.

Wang nodded without looking at him.

"I will be studying all night in my room," said the young man. "Will you return late?"

Wang didn't reply.

"There are two single beds in the room and one desk. If you watch movies on your phone, please use earbuds," said the young man, as they crossed the road.

Wang nodded.

A few minutes later, they went through the front door of the Millenium. The young man showed a card and they passed the security guards, who just looked them up and down. They didn't seem to remember Wang. They took the elevator up to the thirty-third floor. The young man opened the door to his room. It was small. Books were laid out on the floor and on a table.

"You are studying for exams?" said Wang.

"Yes." The young man started tidying up his books.

"You have clean towels?" said Wang.

"Yes, every day. Check the bathroom."

Wang went into the bathroom. He replied to the message from the driver he'd received earlier.

I am delayed, he wrote. Then he sent the message.

After he'd showered, he dressed and opened the small plastic pill container he'd received in Washington. The tablets inside were about the size of a small pimple. He took three out and put them into his trouser pocket. There was nothing else in the pocket.

He looked at the Chinese instructions on the pill container. *WARNING*, it read. *Do Not Exceed the Stated Dose.*

He exited the bathroom and put his jacket on.

"See you later," he called out, as he left the room, knowing full well that he would never see the student again. He paused outside the room, looking down the corridor one way, then the other. He'd swap everything to be in that young man's shoes, to be starting again. Not to be trapped by ambition and desire. And to know what he knew now about life.

54

Vladimir knocked back the vodka. "I don't intend to make a fool of myself, young Katerina, by asking for a trip to your room. If you have a plan for what I can do to help your mission, put it out on the table and I will see what I can do."

Katerina looked sad. Mock sad. She took her phone out, spoke quickly in Russian, telling someone to go home.

"Your boyfriend was waiting to take a picture of me in your room with my trousers down?"

Katerina shook her head. It didn't look convincing.

"I know every trick we play on each other," said Vladimir.

"No tricks. Can you just answer a few questions?"

"Go on."

"We're working on a big cyber op. Do you know about it?"

"I heard we can access their Homeland Security watch lists and some other things."

"We've put a lot of work into this, Vladimir. I hope whatever Moscow has asked you to do doesn't compromise us. We don't need anyone from Moscow messing things up."

"I can see why they selected you for this important job." He looked down at her breasts.

"I'm not an idiot," she said, angrily. "Look at my face." Each word was separate and loud.

He looked up.

"Your reputation made me believe you might help. If you won't, then please, go to hell, fast."

She stood, pushed her chair back.

He stood too.

"Come to my room," he said. "I have an idea how we can help each other."

She put her head to one side.

"How?" she said.

"I will show you."

Twenty minutes later they were in his room. He'd already poured her a large shot of vodka.

"What's the plan?" she said, sitting on the bed.

"I have leverage," he said. "Watch." He took out his phone and tapped at the screen.

55

Manhattan, June 5th, 2020

Rob looked at his screen. *Your wife is waiting for your reply*, was the message.

He looked at Gong Dao. She had her phone in her hand.

"My friend has arrived," she said. "Perhaps you will explain to him why you showed me that picture."

"Who's arrived?"

"You will find out."

A knock echoed. Gong Dao checked herself quickly in the mirror, pushed her hair back behind her ear, then went and opened the door.

"Senator Harmforth, this is Dr. Rob McNeil. He came to see me about his wife, who he thinks died in London."

The senator put his elbow out. He wasn't wearing a mask. Rob was, as was Gong Dao.

"What's going on?" said the senator, a wary look on his face.

"Dr. McNeil wants me to defect," said Gong Dao. "He showed me pictures of my mother."

"Who's making the offer?" said the senator.

"I'm simply passing a message," said Rob.

"Well, you can tell whoever you're working for to back off," said the senator. "Back off now or risk some real powerful players coming down on top of you all."

Rob looked from the senator to Gong Dao. "You two are good friends?" he said.

"I don't care for what you're implying, son. But let's go back to first base. What happened to your wife?"

"I saw her coffin going in to be cremated in London last month, and now I'm being told she's still alive."

"Who told you that?"

"Your friend here, for one."

"What do you know about his wife?" said the senator, looking at Gong Dao.

"Russian State Security services kidnapped her, so they claim. Dr. McNeil is a prominent vaccine researcher. I assume that's why they did it," she said.

The senator went to the antique French-style couch and sat down. He spread his arms and legs wide.

"There you have it, McNeil. What vaccine company do you work for?"

"I work for a research lab in England. Recently we partnered with TOTALVACS."

The senator put his head back. "You're one of Bishop's boys."

Rob didn't answer.

"Well, you better relay a message to your Dr. Bishop that he should call me directly if he wants some background on all this and . . ." he pointed at Rob. "Ask yourself, do you really think the Russians would lie about this?"

Gong Dao shook her head.

Rob's phone buzzed again.

He looked at it. The call ID came up. *Jackie*. It felt as if his heart was trying to get out through his windpipe.

211

He tried to answer the call. He missed the button. His fingers wouldn't work. The room grew small around him. He stabbed at the answer button again and put his phone to his ear. He didn't speak.

"Rob, is that you?" It was Jackie's voice.

He took a step back, put a hand out to hold the nearby wall. Thudding beat in his ears.

"Do what they say, Rob," said Jackie. Her voice shook. She was in danger. His heart responded, beating like a caged animal's.

"Where are you?" said Rob, his voice tense.

"They will release me if you follow their instructions, Rob." She was reading from a script.

"Just tell me where you are."

"I have to go," she said. The call ended.

He tried to call the number back. It didn't connect.

"Who was that?" said the senator.

"My wife, I think," said Rob. He stared at his phone, as if he was seeing it for the first time.

"Be careful, Russians very clever with phone things," said Gong Dao. "But your wife is alive, that is what we heard from two sources, though she may not be the one calling you. They can record her voice and use just what they want, in case she gives anything away."

"What did she say?" said the senator.

"That I'm to follow instructions."

"You've been suckered, son," said the senator.

A knock came from the door. Gong Dao and the senator exchanged glances. She went to the door, looked through the spyhole, and gasped.

She put her hands up and across her chest and stepped back once and then again, and then her head shook

212

from side to side, as if she'd seen something she didn't believe.

She opened her mouth. Her eyes closed and she fell, slumping down, her head missing the coffee table by inches. Rob stepped forward, his hands out to help her.

Gong Dao's arms, body, and legs shook violently.

"I got this," said the senator. He leaned over Gong Dao, pushed her gently on her side, grabbed a cushion from the sofa, and put it under her head.

"Epilepsy?" said Rob.

A loud knock sounded from the door.

"See who it is," said the senator.

Rob went to the door. He looked through the spy hole. Wang Hu was outside. He stepped back. His skin crawled. The expression on Wang's face was not a happy one.

The senator was kneeling beside Gong Dao, who was still convulsing, but not so violently. He stroked her back.

"It's a Chinese Ministry of State Security guy," said Rob, softly.

"Don't open it," said the senator. "It's those bastards have her like this."

"Is she epileptic?" said Rob, bending down.

"Yes."

"Should I call a doctor?"

"I am a doctor. I know what I'm doing," said the senator.

A thud sounded from the door, as if it was being kicked in.

"Call security," said the senator. "The doors are good here, but we need help. Tell them to get up fast, that

Laurence O'Bryan

someone's trying to break into our room." He nodded at the phone on the side table near the window.

Rob went to it, dialed the number for security from the row of numbers on the top of the phone, then asked for someone to come to the room. The thudding at the door continued, getting louder; the door shuddered on its hinges.

"We'll be there in two minutes," came the reply on the phone.

Gong Dao's convulsions had almost stopped. A giant thud from the door made the windows creak. Rob looked around for a weapon. And then there was silence. The only thing he could hear now was the sound of the senator talking in a soothing voice in Chinese.

Gong Dao coughed. She leaned up, came slowly to her feet, and headed for one of the bedrooms with the senator following her.

Rob looked at his phone. It was near seven-thirty. They were supposed to be going back to Washington soon.

It was time to call Faith.

"What's going on?" she asked. He told her about the epileptic fit and about Wang trying to get in.

"It could be a trick," she said.

"It looked real to me. She also claims Jackie's alive." He rubbed a hand across his forehead. "I can't go back to Washington tonight."

There was silence at the other end of the line.

Then Faith spoke. "You're not going to get your wife back," she said. "They're stringing you along. The Chinese are in on it."

"I got a call from Jackie. She sounded alive," said Rob. He'd had his doubts while Jackie had been speaking, but he'd been so happy to hear her voice, so excited, they'd gone away quickly. Now he wasn't so sure.

"I'll call you tomorrow," he said. It had come to him that maybe he should distance himself from Faith if he wanted to get Jackie back. All she ever did was tell him Jackie was dead. She didn't even want to explore the possibility that she was alive. What did he have to lose if he did explore it?

The senator had come back into the room. "Gong Dao will be back with us in a few minutes," he said. He pointed at Rob's phone. "Was that your TOTALVACS friends?"

Rob nodded.

"They're a bunch of fantasists, you know that, right?" said the senator. "They see conspiracies under every fig leaf. You should get a second opinion on everything they tell you."

"I'm not stupid," said Rob.

"Never said you were," said the senator. "But if they really want to help you, they would have told you I'm on a special White House team tasked with helping end this virus BS."

"You are?" said Rob. How come Faith hadn't told him? TOTALVACS had to know this.

A shout and then a loud knocking started up from the door. The senator went to open it. He checked the spyhole first, then swung the door open. The two security guards from the front entrance to the hotel came into the room. One had a taser in his hand, point down.

The senator pointed at Rob. "This man is an intruder. He tried to force himself on the lady staying in this room. We cannot get him to leave," he said.

The security guard raised his taser. It had a yellow nozzle on it.

"Leave this room," said the guard to Rob.

"This is crazy shit," said Rob. He raised his hands high. A blue light flickered at the corner of his eye and an electric pulse, like the kick of a mule, jolted into him, making his jaw open. He fell to the carpet. It was his turn to shake and roll. The pain in his skull and in his bones felt like a blazing fire had been lit inside him.

He saw Gong Dao standing in the doorway to the bedroom. She was smiling. One of the hotel security guards was bending down beside him.

"We take sexual harassment charges at this hotel very seriously," he said. "We will have this man out of your room at once."

56

Vladimir filled their vodka glasses again, this time to the brim. "Katerina, my pussycat, the time for pretense is over." He put a hand on her arm, squeezed it.

"Uncle Vladimir," Katerina smiled, her head to one side. She gripped his hand and twisted it away.

Vladimir replied by placing his other hand on hers and pressing it back onto her other arm.

"I am not your pussycat," hissed Katerina, pulling away.

Vladimir released his hold on her. "Your generation are all bloody snowflakes," he said. "You melt at the slightest provocation."

"Your generation thinks women should be in the bedroom or the kitchen, nowhere else."

He opened his mouth to speak, thought better of it, and downed his vodka shot instead. He raised his empty glass in the air.

"Za zda-ró-vye," he said.

She downed her shot, clinked her empty glass against his.

"Za zda-ró-vye," she said.

"Now that we are both breaking the foreign ministry regulations, I hope we go all the way," said Vladimir.

"All the way to what, Uncle?" said Katerina, her eyes wide and innocent.

Vladimir stood, went to the bed, bent down and looked under it.

"Where is your cameraman boyfriend?" he said.

"Not here," she said.

Vladimir checked the wardrobe and the bathroom. He turned on the taps in the sink and in the shower and motioned for her to join him through the doorway.

When she came in, he whispered in her ear.

"I know your game," he said.

She whispered back. "Do you?"

He looked her in the eyes. They were ice blue, the type that could swallow you whole and eat you before breakfast.

"I work for the motherland," he said. "I can have ten girls like you lined up on their knees every night back in Moscow."

She shook her head as if she didn't care. "Can your mission help mine, Uncle Vladimir? That's all I care about."

"What help do you need?"

"Distractions. Make them think we're focused on the old school stuff."

Vladimir raised a fist high, shook it. "Old school is what I do best. My mission is to bring down the enemies of the motherland." Every word was heartfelt. "Our revenge will be sweet when both our missions succeed. Does that help?"

She reached her hand up to curl it around his neck.

His phone buzzed. He rocked back on his heels and leaned against the tiled wall as he pulled the phone out of his pocket.

57

Wang had his hand to his mouth. Had he gone too far? He'd walked back to the room of the young man who'd brought him into the hotel. He'd let Wang in without a smile and had put his earphones back in his ear and returned to his desk to study.

Wang's mind raced. If he couldn't break Gong Dao's door down, another way to make progress might be to find something out about what she was doing here in Manhattan. He knew he was risking everything, but he couldn't let all chance of winning her go. His doggedness had helped him rise. Now it was threatening to break him.

He couldn't turn away. No chance.

He texted the driver who had been sent for him to wait another two hours.

Then he called the number of the woman from the *Eye of the Ocean* in Beijing. After five rings, the call was answered.

"Mr. Wang Hu, is everything OK with your room?"

"Yes," said Wang.

He went to the bathroom, locked the door. "I need to know what mission a Ms. Gong Dao, working for our embassy in Washington DC, is engaged in."

There was a pause at the other end of the line.

"We will expect full support from you, when we ask, is that understood?"

"Yes, you will have my full support."

"Please wait for the information. It will arrive on your phone in our app. Check it out," said the voice.

Wang closed the call, found the app, downloaded it, and waited. He tapped at the wall as he did, like a woodpecker.

58

"And don't come back," said one of the security guards, as he pushed Rob out into the street.

"I was invited into that room," shouted Rob, despair in his voice.

He'd been manhandled into the corridor. They'd held him under the arms as he shook, still recovering from the taser, and had half walked him, half dragged him into the elevator. Then they held him tight while they descended and force-marched out into the street.

The security guard had asked his name in the elevator and if he was staying in the hotel. He'd given his name but had denied he had a room. He didn't want Faith thrown out too.

"Don't come back," said the guard, as he stood at the main door, shaking his head, his arms folded.

His brain was still recovering from the shock of the taser. His body was mostly back under his control, but his teeth felt weird, as if they'd been loosened and his breath was still coming fast.

"You just took her word over mine?" he shouted to the security guards.

"You're lucky we don't call the cops and have you arrested for harassment and trespassing," said the guard. "You're lucky the woman upstairs doesn't want to press charges, so just get the hell out of here." He pointed at Rob. "It's our experience that when a woman accuses a man of forcing his way into her room, she's telling the truth. Why would she lie?" The guards backed up and the automatic glass doors of the hotel closed.

Rob turned in a circle. The plaza was almost empty. What would he do now? The plan to get Gong Dao to defect had failed, but did that really matter? She was already working with the White House. And none of that was important, compared to the call he'd received from Jackie. He took his phone out and replied to the text he'd received earlier from Jackie.

I will do whatever you want. But I need to meet you. No more videos. No more calls.

He sent the message and called Faith.

"I've been thrown out of the hotel," he said. "But I gave Gong Dao your message."

"Where are you?"

"Outside the hotel."

"We'll be there in five. Our driver came early," she said.

The Chevy pulled up at the intersection about two minutes later. Rob got in the back. Faith was in the other seat.

"What happened about Gong Dao?" she asked.

"She's working with the senator. He said he's on a special task force from the White House. But you know that, right? You know everything about him."

"That senator is on half a dozen task forces, Rob. And he claims to be on others no one has ever heard of."

Rob shook his head. "Well, Gong Dao is epileptic, and she's avoiding our friend Wang and she's working with the senator who said we should back off," he said.

"Wow," said Faith.

"And it looks like Wang really wanted to get into her room, like he's obsessed with her, and she didn't want to see him."

"That won't help his career," said Faith.

"I also got a call from Jackie." He told Faith what had happened.

"This is all driving me crazy, Faith." He held his stomach. It felt weird, almost as if he might vomit.

"Don't believe any of it," she said.

His phone buzzed. A message had come in.

You are invited to the Russian Embassy in Washington DC at 9 a.m. tomorrow. The Russian Embassy is committed to helping families in distress find their loved ones.

He let his breath out, held the phone out for Faith to read the message.

"I have to get back to Washington," he said.

"Don't get your hopes up, Rob. The Russians are not straight players."

"What can they do to me in their embassy?"

"They can play games with your head. Demand to see her somewhere else."

Rob looked at his phone. They were driving slowly through mostly empty streets.

Faith began texting furiously.

Rob sent a reply to the message.

Can we do the meeting anywhere else in DC?

A minute later a reply came.

Not possible. Do not be late.

Laurence O'Bryan

"How soon can we be in Washington?" he asked.

"You go to Washington. I'm staying here," said Faith. She tapped the driver's shoulder. "Let me out."

Rob put his hand up. "We should drop you where you're going," he said.

"I have another vehicle behind," she said. She pointed with her thumb. Rob looked out the back window. A similar black Chevy was about a half block behind.

As Faith got out, she said to the driver. "Make sure he gets to Washington tonight."

"Yes, ma'am," replied the driver.

"Someone will be watching the embassy, Rob. They'll probably try to get you to do something, maybe show you another video to prove she's alive. Don't believe it. In fact, I recommend you don't go there. But if you insist on finding out that they're just stringing you along, so be it. We ain't going to stop you. And when you do get away from them, go in to TOTALVACS and call me."

She leaned back in as she was about to close the Chevy door. "I really hope tomorrow ends any doubt once and for all you have about what they're telling you."

She slammed the Chevy door.

59

Vladimir pulled on his shirt. Katerina was in the shower. She had asked him about every scar on his front and back. He'd only explained a few. There were some things he never wanted to talk about. His phone buzzed again. A series of messages awaited him.

Be at the embassy by eight, was one.

Special guest arriving at nine, was another.

He opened the bathroom door and put his head in. "I have to go," he shouted.

"Good luck," replied Katerina from the steamed-up shower cubicle.

He didn't reply. He left the room, making sure the door was locked after exiting. He needed sleep. Tomorrow would be a busy day.

He was back in his room thirty minutes later. He called the security officer at the embassy.

"Everything ready for my guest?" he asked.

"Yes," came the reply. "We are always happy to arrange reconciliation meetings."

"Good, this one will be extra special."

60

Wang finished his shower and had opened the *Eye of the Ocean* app. He sat on the edge of his bed going through the various menus available from the restaurant chain around the world, the pictures of celebrities at their restaurants, and the notice board for placing reviews of restaurants or dishes. All the reviews there were stellar.

The young man whose room he was in turned abruptly, yanked his earphones off, and said, "Two men are on their way up to our floor. They asked about me. They must be looking for you."

Wang looked over the young man's shoulder. In the corner of the screen, he had a view of the lobby downstairs. Another small window showed two Chinese men in suits coming up in an elevator.

"You have maybe twenty seconds to get to the fire escape stairs. That way," said the young man, pointing down the corridor.

"And you?" said Wang.

"They aren't looking for me," said the young man. "I will visit with a friend in the room opposite until they're gone." He shook his head. "She won't want you in her room."

The two of them exited the hotel room together. The young man must have had a pass card to his girlfriend's room, as he was gone when Wang looked around, before he opened the door to the fire escape stairs. Then he went down, taking the steps in jumps. When he'd gone down six floors, he heard a noise from up above.

He stopped jumping and pushed open the door on that floor, closing it gently behind him. It was probably the driver and one of the other men from the embassy. They most likely wanted to force him to come with them back to Washington.

He walked slowly down the corridor. His phone buzzed. A message had come in on the restaurant app. It was an image of him arriving at their restaurant in Manhattan. He stopped, opened the message. Below it, there was text.

Project Name: Poison the Wells. 1. Recruit individuals who will spread misinformation inside the United States, 2. Identify individuals willing to demonstrate on the streets and who need financial assistance.

He read it again, then scrolled back to the top of the message. The image was gone. He reloaded the screen. The entire message was gone.

A shout echoed down the corridor. Two men from the Chinese Embassy in black suits, with red ties, were walking toward him with smiles on their faces.

"We are happy to have found you, Mr. Wang Hu," said one of the men.

They did indeed look happy. Wang glanced over his shoulder. The elevator was some way off. Running was not an option. He had to pretend he'd just been delayed.

He turned and raised his hands in greeting. "Where have you been?" he asked.

"Looking for you," said the driver. "We must get you back to Washington."

"Let's go then," he said.

227

Laurence O'Bryan

Thirty minutes later they were exiting the Lincoln Tunnel and moving fast along I-95. Not long after, they were on the New Jersey Turnpike, which was almost empty—a highly unusual sight for a Friday evening, which would usually have been bumper to bumper traffic with people heading out of the city.

Wang Hu sat in the back. The driver and the other embassy official were in the front.

His phone buzzed insistently. A new message from the *Eye of the Ocean* app had arrived. The buzz it created was so loud the official in the front turned around to stare at him with curiosity written all over his face.

Wang opened the app. The message was a picture of the restaurant chain's famous Five-Spice Duck soup, which it bragged about on its social media sites.

The image had Chinese characters embedded in it. He opened the pic. It was a fortune-cookie message.

Your journey must end or you will pay the final price.

He glanced up. The official was looking at him again, turning in his seat, smiling with his mouth only. The bulge in the man's jacket was more prominent now. Not many from the embassy staff would be allowed out with a weapon. The only reason to have one would be to use it.

61

Faith leaned back. "How far ahead are they?" she asked. She undid the button on her black jacket and took a moment to close her eyes and enjoy the comfortable and enveloping rear seat of the Chevy.

"Ten minutes," said the driver. "You want me to use the blue light?"

"No," she said. "Just close the distance slowly. Have we got satellite tracking on them?"

"Yes, ma'am," said the other young State Department official in the vehicle, sitting in the front with the driver. He turned and showed an iPad screen to Faith.

"We set up a tracking priority for the vehicle. We have satellite and ground cameras."

"Your name is?" said Faith.

"Noah Oliver, ma'am."

"And McNeil is where, Mr. Oliver?" she said.

"McNeil's twenty minutes ahead of our target, ma'am."

"Hold on," said Noah. He peered hard at the screen he was holding.

"The target has pulled off at Mile Post 92.9; that's Woodbridge." He blinked, peered closer at the text on his screen. "That's the Thomas Edison service area. They may have pulled in for gas."

"Do we have air support?" asked Faith.

"We have a Huey in the air from McGuire AFB. They're staying out of sight, tracking us, and will only deploy if we call them in."

"Has our translation unit confirmed the messages received by the target?"

"Yes, ma'am."

"And we have confirmation that one of the Chinese officials in the vehicle is a member of their Sea Dragon Commando unit?"

"Yes, ma'am. And, ma'am, we're coming up to the Thomas Edison service area. Shall we turn in?"

"Yes," said Faith.

62

"I'll be finished quickly," said Wang. He pointed at the Sunco gas station near the concrete-colored rest area and restaurant building.

"You get gas," he said.

"No need, we wait for you outside," said the official riding shotgun. He pointed at an empty space for the driver to pull up where they could watch the front and side of the building.

The driver pulled the car into it. Wang got out. He looked back as he neared the building. The driver had gotten out too and was following him. Perhaps he needed the restrooms, but he was also clearly watching Wang.

The only time Wang had ever heard of a Ministry of State Security official being watched this closely was when they were about to be exposed for something, sent to re-education camp, or even one of the special prisons for security officials.

Those prisons made the one he'd visited in Wuhan the month before look like holiday camps. He'd interrogated a corrupt party official in one of them. All the men he'd seen in the camp had stumps for teeth, some had an empty eye socket, and every face had been wrapped in a gray despair.

Laurence O'Bryan

He needed to find out what they had on him, so he could clear his name. He would not be able to do that from a prison cell.

He walked fast past the restrooms, looking for the back way out. He turned a corner and was faced with a long empty corridor with closed signs on shops on either side. Only one of the restaurants in the main area behind him was open, and only for takeaways. He spotted a door with an emergency handle and walked fast to it. He pushed at the door and went through as an alarm sounded.

He stood behind the door as it opened, and waited.

63

"Pull over at the far end," said Faith, pointing past the vehicle they'd been following.

"What do you think; just a rest stop?" asked Noah.

"No idea," said Faith. "Anything could happen."

"I'll call in support," said the driver.

"Don't do that," said Faith. "We haven't got an incident yet. "I'm not getting air support in for a trip to the john."

"Shall I go inside?" said Noah.

"You go in the front, scope the john. I'll check around the back, just in case they exit to another vehicle. I don't want to lose them."

She didn't say there'd been an incident at a similar service area two years before, that had nearly cost her position at State. That time, a foreign embassy official was wanted for questioning about a DUI with multiple deaths. He'd escaped by the back door. He was never heard of again. And the families never got closure. She blamed herself for that.

The driver turned to her. "I'll go with you, ma'am. You need backup."

"Nope, you stay here. Watch their vehicle."

Faith pressed the thumb-lock release on her Sig Sauer P320 holster. She kept her right hand inside her jacket, an inch from her weapon as she walked through the car park. There weren't many vehicles, but there were enough to indicate the area which would have families wandering around and possibly young children exploring around the back.

A honk from a truck made her turn her head. She couldn't see where it had come from. Cars were passing fast along I-95. She could smell gas fumes and the thrum of vehicles filled her ears. She stayed a good fifty feet from the building as she went around, to give her a line of sight, and as she turned the corner at the side of the building, she looked back at their vehicle.

Its black windows gave nothing away. Should she have called for backup? Yeah, but how long would that take to arrive? And there was probably nothing going down here. Right? Yeah, right.

She walked past other vehicles, looking for the back exit out of the rest area. There had to be one. Fire exits were mandatory in service areas.

There was an open field to the right now, and a short line of straggly trees at the back of the service area.

A couple of wooden picnic tables waited under the trees. A high wooden partition separated the picnic area from the rear of the building. She walked toward it.

As she neared it, she shivered. Something in her bones didn't like this. It was exactly the same type of day as her previous experience at a service station incident. The sky was the same, rapidly darkening blue, and the tension inside her was the same, like a wire being turned and tightened.

She was nearly at the partition. A shout rang out. She put her hand on her weapon and rounded the corner.

64

Washington DC, June 5th, 2020

Vladimir reached his apartment building as the evening shadows were lengthening. Sitting outside the building stood a black Chevy with darkened windows. He'd have to walk near it to get to the front entrance. He looked around. There'd be no witnesses if someone was going to pull him in.

He kept a good distance from the vehicle and his eyes roaming as he passed it. As he did, a back window rolled down and a voice called out.

"Vladimir, good to see you," said the voice.

He stopped, looked in, and squinted to see the person in the shadows inside the vehicle.

"Dr. Bishop, it's been a long time."

Bishop was wearing a blue face mask, but there was no mistaking him.

"Seven years almost exactly," said Bishop. "I have a message for you, Vladimir." He motioned with a finger for Vladimir to come closer.

Vladimir did and leaned down. Then he spat on the ground nearby.

"Make it quick," he said. "I'm a busy man and I don't forget your tricks."

Bishop made a scoffing noise. "If you value your ability to come and go in the United States, you will lay off our man, McNeil," he said.

Vladimir laughed scornfully. "They send a big fish like you for this message, eh? Is that it?"

Bishop shook his head. "We're prepared to share our research, Vladimir." There was a sad note to his voice, as if he didn't expect the offer to be taken up. "I represent TOTALVACS these days and you can tell your masters that if they want to develop an early vaccine with McNeil's ideas, tested properly, they should contact me." He leaned forward, made a fist.

"But if you mess with McNeil's head and he stops working for us, or causes us any mischief, we will never cooperate with you on his vaccine, and you will be barred from coming back to the United States."

Vladimir put his face down to Bishop's level.

"You think you are in charge of everything, yes? Ha, you people have no idea what's coming." He bared his teeth. "I don't do what I'm told by a Pindo, who will do anything to bring down Mother Russia. You tried your tricks in two thousand and thirteen. We're ready for you this time."

"I will also have you barred from Canada, Vladimir. Your daughter's in Toronto, right?"

Vladimir shrugged, but the anger inside him was ready to blow. He knew, though, that he could not show it. He hadn't seen his daughter in twenty years, but always, at the back of his mind, he'd hoped they might reconcile. He followed her progress.

"We hear she's looking for tenure at her university. I hope the university authorities make a quick decision." Bishop pointed at Vladimir again. "You need to play a straight game, Vladimir."

Laurence O'Bryan

Vladimir leaned down. It was a good thing Bishop was wearing a face mask. There was spittle coming out of Vladimir's mouth as he spoke.

"Don't threaten me. Your relationship with the truth is worse than ours." He made a dismissive noise. "And do what you like to my daughter, I don't care and I never have." He turned and walked fast toward the apartment building.

He hoped what he'd said about his daughter would get them to her leave her alone. If they thought for one second that they could use her as a lever against him, she would be under their thumb forever.

It was the reason he hadn't contacted his daughter or her mother for twenty years. When your personal records are available to your friends and your enemies too, you cannot have a family and live in peace for even one day.

It was even better to have a family member tortured to death to prove this, than to have all your children, your wife and her family tortured one after the other, each time your enemies wanted you to do something.

He slammed the front door of the apartment building and watched as Bishop's Chevy moved off and headed downtown.

65

Wang stood still as the steel fire exit door of the rest area opened, slowly. The man opening it was being super cautious.

Wang leaned to the side, then jumped at the door with his shoulder leading. It sprang inward. A grunt of pain followed. He pulled the door open to reveal the driver holding his head. Blood seeped from a wound on the man's forehead. His first instinct was to step back, look around, check if there were any other dangers. The corridor beyond the driver was empty, and both the man's hands were at his head. He was down, almost on his knees.

"What was that for?" said the driver, plaintively.

Wang blinked. Had he misjudged? The man had no obvious weapon. He could have easily just been following him.

He reached down to help the driver to his feet.

The driver's hand swung up. A thin-bladed gutting knife glistened.

"Traitor," hissed the driver, as the knife plunged into his stomach. It might have come out the other side if Wang hadn't pulled his body back at the last moment.

The pain was like a cold icy shard impaling him

The driver had a snarl on his face. Wang knew what was coming. How had he been so stupid? One more push upwards and the knife would cut through his heart.

A hollow thud echoed. The driver's forehead exploded. Bone and wet brain showered into Wang's face. His stomach felt like a water balloon that had burst. His thighs felt wet.

He fell back, the knife came out, sucking at his skin. He shrieked, pressed his hands to his stomach as hot blood pumped out of the wound.

"Emergency, ambulance needed fast, Thomas Edison Service Area I-95," a voice shouted. He looked up. Silhouetted against the sunset stood Faith Gordon, the United States State Department official he had released in Beijing. In her hand was a black pistol, a sliver of gray smoke drifting from the barrel.

She leaned down.

"Wang Hu, I hereby place you in protective custody as you are at high risk of being harmed. Do you agree to this?"

Wang didn't reply.

"Do you agree to this?"

Everything went dark. A metallic taste filled his mouth.

66

Vladimir looked at his watch. It was five to nine. The room, deep in the Russian Embassy building, was small, gray, and windowless. The status of the operation was unofficial and deniable. On the table in front of him lay a form, facing away.

Family Re-unification Obligations Form, it read in English on one side. If you turned it over, it said the same thing in Russian.

He placed a thin biro at the side of the form and looked at his watch again. They'd be here soon. He pressed his right fist into his left palm. Bishop and TOTALVACS and all the rest of them would get what they deserved. What did it matter if he twisted rules to get a good job done?

A knock sounded from the door.

"Come in," he said, loudly.

A dark-haired woman opened the door. Behind her stood Dr. Robert McNeil. He looked around the room as he came in.

"Where is my wife?" said McNeil, angrily.

"Sit down if you want to see her," said Vladimir.

The door slammed shut.

"If this is some trick, I swear I'll make you pay," said McNeil.

"This is no trick. Please read the form in front of you and sign it."

McNeil had a pained expression on his face. He was slightly stooped too, as if getting ready to run. Vladimir had seen men who looked like this in corrective labor camps. Usually they were the men who had expectations of leaving the camp soon and had become twisted inside as their expectations ate at them.

McNeil picked up the form, read it, but did not sit. When he was finished, he waved it toward Vladimir.

"I'm not going to sign this crap," he shouted. "You must be joking."

"Please, sit down first and then we will proceed," said Vladimir.

McNeil tried to move the steel chair on the other side of the table. It was screwed to the floor. He sat with an annoyed grunt and threw the form on the table.

"What's happening. Where's my wife?" said McNeil.

"Sign the form, Dr. McNeil. This is easy." Vladimir gave a quick smile.

McNeil picked up the form, read it slowly this time, his lips pressed tight. "I hope this is worth it," he said.

"I do too," said Vladimir.

McNeil picked up the biro. "Is my wife in the building? This form talks about bringing families together." His hand hovered over the bottom of the form.

"I cannot answer any questions until the form has been signed, Dr. McNeil." Vladimir kept his expression stiff. Compliance was required. Compliance was the key.

McNeil let out a groan and signed.

Vladimir took the form from him. "You must understand that you have agreed to take no legal action in this or any jurisdiction against the Russian state and that you agree our only concern at all times in dealing with you is to bring families together who have been separated."

"I've signed your goddamn form. Get on with it," said McNeil. "Your ass is covered."

"Wait here," said Vladimir. He stood, headed for the door.

"Stop," shouted McNeil.

Vladimir turned, his hand near the door. "Please be patient, Dr. McNeil."

"Is this all some evil trick? Tell me now if it is. I've signed your form. Let me out of this misery."

Vladimir pulled his phone out and tapped at it. He looked at the video on the screen and turned the phone to McNeil.

"See you soon, I hope," said Jackie, McNeil's wife, visible on the screen. Then she sobbed. The video went black.

McNeil raised a fist. "What the hell are you doing to her?" he shouted.

"All your questions will be answered soon. Wait here," said Vladimir.

He exited the room, closed the door, and locked it from the outside. He gave a thumbs up to the armed guard. The man acknowledged the gesture, then went back to his position, to attention, at the side of the door.

67

Faith went in through the main door of the hospital. A security guard put his hand up and pointed at a sign which said *No Visitors*. Faith pulled her badge out from her pocket.

"Official business," she said.

The guard pointed at the sterilizing station. "Please ensure you wear a mask at all times and sterilize your hands regularly, ma'am."

"Will do," said Faith, as he squeezed sterilizer onto her hands. She adjusted her mask at the ears to sit tighter.

"Where is the secure ward?"

"Third floor, turn left," said the guard, his voice muffled behind his bulky white mask.

Faith rode the elevator up. She rubbed lint from her shirt. The nearby motel she'd stayed at was basic, but it was all she needed.

A State Department backup unit had arrived soon after a New Jersey State police cruiser, as she was holding Wang's wound closed. An ambulance arrived a minute after that. She'd used her jacket to staunch Wang's wound and told a medic to throw it away as she stumbled to her feet.

It was not appropriate for her to accompany Wang to the hospital, as she had been involved in the incident, but she'd found out where they were taking him after giving an

244

initial statement to three different officers: one from New Jersey, one from the State Department task force, and one to an officer from the New Jersey Medical Examiner's office, who arrived as she was leaving the scene.

The other man in the Chinese Embassy vehicle had been arrested, she found out later, but was pleading diplomatic immunity and claiming he didn't even speak English. The Chinese Embassy had been contacted but denied all knowledge of the incident. They had asked for Wang's location and had used the term "personal dispute," to characterize what had happened.

Wang had been alive when they put him in the ambulance, probably thanks to Faith holding the wound tight, so one of the emergency crew said. When she called the hospital later that evening, they said his condition was stable.

Now all she had to do was find out what the hell had happened and even more critically, if there was any chance of getting him to defect and spill the beans on what the Chinese state had been up to, both in Wuhan and here in the United States.

There had to be a lot he could tell them. An offer of immunity and a relocation package could help ensure that this moment became a breakthrough in the investigation into what the Chinese security services had been up to before and during the early stages of the Coronavirus pandemic.

The world deserved to know not only how it started, but why the Chinese had allowed their citizens to fly to the United States and elsewhere when they knew the Coronavirus flew with them. Was that their plan? If it was, it came very close to bio-warfare.

She nodded at the two State Department security officers standing by the door to a room, showed her badge, and pushed in. The State Department would have to make a call soon, to decide whether to allow the Chinese Embassy official waiting at the front of the building since 4 a.m., could visit Wang.

The excuse of protective custody wouldn't work if Wang was likely to refuse it. More senior embassy officials were probably on the way too. A diplomatic incident was brewing. The whole thing could go either way. If Wang didn't cooperate, a huge opportunity to see inside the Chinese State's response to the virus would be lost.

She pushed open the door. Wang looked to be asleep. Monitoring equipment beeped quietly. The lights were down and there was a stink of disinfectant. A wide bandage covered Wang's exposed stomach.

She stood by Wang's bed, her hand hovering near his on the crisp white sheet. Her superior officer had only agreed to allow her a short visit, because Wang might recognize her as the person who'd saved his life and agree to protective custody. It helped that she also spoke Mandarin.

She looked down at him. His expression was peaceful. Was there any possibility the attack on Wang was personal? No. Faith hated coincidences. A personal attack would definitely be a coincidence happening at the same time as she was trying to connect with him.

A nurse came into the room. Faith told her who she was, and that she needed to speak to Wang, briefly.

"Was he awake at all?" she asked the nurse.

"He's been awake a couple of times, so he's not unconscious. He might wake if you speak louder," said the nurse as she checked the readings on the monitoring equipment. Then she left the room.

Faith said his name. "Wang." Then she said it louder. Then louder again.

His eyelids flickered.

"Wang, it's me, Faith." She bent toward him. "Can you hear me?"

His eyes were closed again. She said his name again. His eyelids opened. He spoke in Mandarin as he looked around.

"Where am I?"

She told him. His gaze stayed on her.

"You saved me," he said.

She nodded. "Yes, and I need you to make a decision right now, Wang. Your embassy wants to visit you, take custody of you most likely. And move you somewhere more under their control." She leaned down closer, adjusted her mask at the ears. "We can place you in protective custody and work out a great deal for you, if you cooperate with the United States government. What do you think?"

A wince of pain crossed his face.

"Which will it be?" asked Faith. "Go with your embassy people or let the United States government look after you?"

He looked up at her, examining her eyes.

"You must decide now," said Faith.

68

Washington DC, June 6th, 2020

Vladimir opened the door of the interview room. McNeil had been pacing around the room for the past twenty minutes. It was time.

"Where is she?" asked Rob.

"If you mean your wife Jackie, I again must ask you to be patient, Dr. McNeil."

Rob took a step toward him with his fists up, his head shaking. "You can't do this. This is torture," he shouted.

Vladimir didn't flinch. He was used to facing angry men.

"If you attack me, this meeting ends and you will be thrown out of this building on your backside," he said.

Rob stood two feet from him, his breath a growl. "I know you're playing games with me. You are some evil bastard."

"Is that so," said Vladimir. He raised a hand. The door of the room opened. A woman's voice called out.

"Rob, do what he says, please."

"Jackie," shouted Rob. He stormed to the door. It closed before he reached it.

He swung around. "Another of your evil tricks, you bastard," he said, his tone full of anger

248

Vladimir took his phone out of his pocket, tapped at it. He showed the screen to Rob. A woman was standing in a corridor, just like the one outside the room they were in. She had her head down. Two guards dressed like the security guards in the embassy stood near the woman. She had her back to the camera.

Rob grabbed for the phone, held Vladimir's hand in a vice-like grip, and pulled the phone to him. His mouth opened. He let out a groan of rage. He released Vladimir's hand and stood back.

"What do you want?" he said.

Vladimir opened his arms wide. "The truth is what we want, that's all. The same as you."

"What truth?" said Rob. His face was red, his mouth contorted. Vladimir had seen such faces before, when they were forcing people to do things in Afghanistan. Rob might be near to breaking. Good. And if he didn't, the men outside would be waiting for him with open arms.

"The truth we want is about the swine flu epidemic in Russia in two thousand and nine. You were with a British university then. You were a research assistant to a professor doing gain-of-function research on flu viruses, making them even more deadly."

Rob didn't reply.

"One of our scientists, who you met in Moscow, remembered you from that time. No paper was ever produced on the work, but we know your research was all passed to the British military and then to the Americans. This is right, yes?" He pointed at Rob. "Speak the truth, now."

Rob pressed his lips together, stared at Vladimir. A vein in his forehead had come out. It was moving like a snake.

"Yes, yes, it is true," said Rob, defiantly. "But we broke no laws."

"No laws at that time, but your research could easily have been used to create batches of swine flu, and easily transported, and spread around Ukraine by even one person in the pay of the British Government. Am I right?"

Rob nodded. "It's possible, yes. But why would anyone do such a thing?" He shook his head. "Why do people in Russia always have to blame someone else for their woes?"

Vladimir leaned back and laughed. "Do you know your history?" he asked. "The United States and United Kingdom have been meddling in our affairs for a very long time, including direct military intervention, feet on the ground." He pointed at Rob. "That's something we haven't done to you, yet."

"Can I see my wife now?" said McNeil.

Vladimir pointed at the chair McNeil had been sitting in. The man was cooperating. It was time to get the business done.

"Yes, in time, now sit. We need to get something on tape."

"Get what on tape?" said Rob. The vein in his forehead was pulsing now, almost as if it might burst.

"Not about your swine flu work, Dr. McNeil, don't worry. Your professional reputation will not be trashed."

Rob went to the table but did not sit.

"What then?"

Vladimir sat on his side of the table. Rob was holding the back of his own chair. Vladimir pointed at it, held his arm stiff in the air. After a minute of near silence, with only the sound of their breathing and a distant whirr from the air conditioning, Rob sat.

"Tell me what you want," he said.

"Is your friend Faith Gordon, working for the campaign of former Vice President Biden?" asked Vladimir.

Rob guffawed. "Are you serious? That's what you want—something on Biden?"

Vladimir kept his face still. "Just the truth, McNeil, that's what we want." He pointed at the black camera pod in the corner of the ceiling. "Admit that you have been delaying your vaccine because of input from someone working with Biden and you will get to see your wife. That's fair, yes? The truth will set you free, yes?" Vladimir tried to keep a straight face and not smirk.

Rob's face had gone white. His breathing was heavy enough to be heard. This was it. The moment he would break.

Rob came to his feet, licked his lips, raised his fists, and came toward Vladimir.

69

Faith leaned down. Wang was speaking softly in Mandarin.

"Say that again?" said Faith.

"We poison the wells . . ." His voice trailed off.

"What?"

"Good poison," said Wang softly. Then he relaxed back, as if he'd revealed something momentous.

"What do you mean?" Faith asked. She knew the phrase. It was well known as the solution to rebellious tribes advocated by the original warlords of Manchuria. But what did Wang mean?

"You know Vice President Biden?" whispered Wang.

Faith didn't reply for half a minute. Her work with Biden's team had been limited, and she was not allowed to speak of it. How did he know?

Wang blinked. "I want you to send him a message."

A noise in the corridor, a shout, distracted her. Faith looked around. Was that someone shouting in Mandarin?

She looked back down at Wang. "You must answer right now. Do you want the protection of the United States government?"

Wang looked forlorn. "Will you get a message to Biden?"

252

Faith smiled.

"Yes," she said.

Wang nodded. "What else you do?" he said.

"We can provide you immunity from prosecution. You can start a new life anywhere in the world. You can disappear. But you must cooperate fully. We expect you to tell us every little detail of what your country and your Ministry of State Security has been up to, and all your internal protocols and passwords. Everything."

He smiled up at her.

"Shall I tell your embassy officials to leave?"

He nodded.

"There will be paperwork to sign," she said.

He shrugged.

70

"You bastard," Rob shouted, as he leaned over the table and swung his fist. Vladimir went back in his chair. It went over, clattering, taking him away from Rob's fist and onto the floor. A crack sounded from the door to the corridor as it swung open and smashed against the wall.

A second later, Rob's arms were pinioned.

"Throw him out," shouted Vladimir, getting to his feet. "He is to talk to no one else here."

The guards pushed Rob out the door. They hustled him down the corridor and through another door, with Vladimir behind, watching. A shout filled the corridor as he was pushed out.

"What happened?" It was a female voice. It was Rob's wife's voice. He turned his head, but then he was through a door and being pushed up a long concrete ramp. At the end of the ramp, a steel door waited. It swung open as they approached. Garbage cans stood in a row.

The men pushed Rob through a mesh gate. He was outside the embassy. They closed the gate with a bang behind him.

A dark blue Ford Taurus stood parked nearby. Two men in windcheaters with the letters FBI written on them jumped out as Rob walked away from the embassy. They reached Rob within a few seconds.

He was about to complain about his treatment in the embassy when one of them pulled out handcuffs, which gleamed in the sunlight. To his shock, they grabbed him. His wrists were in the cuffs before he could do anything.

"Dr. Robert McNeil, under The Espionage Act, Title 18 of the US code you are hereby charged with conveying information to a foreign power," said one of the men.

Two other FBI agents had appeared from somewhere. They had hands near their holsters, as if expecting trouble.

"This is crazy," shouted Rob. "You saw me being thrown out of the embassy. That was because I didn't cooperate. What the hell am I being arrested for?"

"You have the right to remain silent, Dr. McNeil. Anything you say may be used against you in a court of law. You have the right to have an attorney present during questioning, and to have one appointed to represent you," said the officer who had cuffed him. "Do you understand these rights?"

"Yes, of course," said Rob.

He was taken toward the Ford Taurus. His head was held down as he was pushed into the back. The door slammed. A thick Perspex block separated the front and the back of the vehicle. As they pulled away, he looked back at the embassy. Through the bars of the gate, he could see Vladimir. He was smiling.

"Bastard," he whispered.

71

Washington DC, June 6th, 2020

As soon as she arrived, Faith went to the restaurant of the TOTALVACS building. She needed coffee. Wang was already on his way to a secure military hospital in Camden, New Jersey. His interrogation proper would start later that day, confined to short sessions.

The normal procedure would be to wait until he'd partially recovered from his wounds, but time was of the essence. A live investigation of Chinese intelligence operations inside the United States was ongoing. They had to know everything about the Chinese *poison the wells* operation.

She sipped her coffee while reading her classified emails.

One press release claimed that the phase three trial of Rob's vaccine had hit the twenty-five thousand volunteer mark with fifty percent having already received a first dose, and of those twenty-five percent in the critical racial minority categories. It was the fastest phase three TOTALVACS had ever undertaken.

Fifty percent of the recipients would be given a saline placebo, the release stated. Each recipient had also received an app to monitor their health on a variety of metrics four times a day. Those without a smartphone had been issued one. It was the most closely monitored trial phase ever in the United States. So, the press release claimed.

But Faith knew that producing and testing a vaccine were only the first stages in the process of getting the public to take it. The vaccine testing process had to be open to scrutiny, and the results had to show that the vaccine was free from all but the most minor side effects.

She looked across the room. One of the PR team for TOTALVACS had come in. He was smiling. The TOTALVACS share price had probably taken a jump. Most of the employees at TOTALVACS had share options. Any jump mattered. A big jump mattered a lot.

She looked up when she heard her name being called. Bishop was coming toward her.

"Good work with Wang Hu," he said.

"Thank you, sir," she said. She sat up straighter.

"Did you hear that your friend McNeil has been taken into custody by the FBI?" he asked.

"Yeah, I knew that was coming," she said. "If he shared anything with the Russians he'll be in big trouble."

"He won't admit it, but they'll find out," he said.

Faith nodded, didn't reply. It would not do any good to show any emotional attachment to McNeil. She had no idea what he was going to admit to.

"What are you doing about Gong Dao?" Bishop asked.

"I'm meeting her for a late lunch."

"Good call. We need to keep the Chinese Embassy people calm. We don't want retaliation against our embassy in Beijing. They will be hopping mad about their driver getting his skull blown open."

"Gong Dao asked to interview me as part of their incident investigation process." Faith shrugged. "It's quick,

Laurence O'Bryan

but understandable, so I passed it up the line. Internal affairs agreed with me. We have to show them we have nothing to hide. I had to shoot that man. He was about to kill someone. Better they hear it straight from me than think we're making it up."

"You'll have backup with you?"

"Sure."

"You're a brave woman letting them see your face."

"They have me tagged for it already. They must have tapped into the camera system at the service area. They knew my name too. Best to be straight with them about this one."

"Wang slipping away through their fingers will piss them off," said Bishop.

She shrugged. "That's another story."

"Be careful when you meet her. She's supposed to be a piece of work." Bishop stood. "I'll make sure you get a commendation for all this," he said.

"Thank you, sir."

He turned back to Faith as he was about to leave.

"Do you think the Russians faked McNeil's wife's death and brought someone that looked like her into the United States? It all looks like one of their stunts to me."

"They are bastards." Faith shook her head.

"They certainly messed with his head," said Bishop. Then he was gone.

Faith finished her coffee. She headed for the office visiting government officials had been allocated in the TOTALVACS building. There were so many countries vying for access to TOTALVACS products, it was essential that a number of interested government departments had their own room in the building.

258

When she opened her laptop in the corner office, she saw an urgent email. It was from the lead investigator who had taken over the interrogation of Wang Hu.

She looked around. No one else was in yet. She called the investigator using the encrypted call app.

"You're not going to believe this," were his first words.

72

"Where are you taking me?" said Rob. "I demand my rights."

One of the men in the front turned to him. "I'm told a million people around the world are going to die from this virus, Dr. McNeil. They demand their rights too."

Rob sat back. They drove through the streets of Washington, then waited outside a gray eight-story office block while two red and black metal access-blockers lowered in front of a ramp down into the building. They turned onto the ramp as soon as they could.

"Welcome to FBI Headquarters," said the driver. They went down two levels and drove through an underground car park until they reached an elevator where two men in blue uniforms were waiting. Both had navy blue face masks on.

One opened the door for Rob and motioned for him to get out.

Rob stepped out. The man held his handcuffed wrists. The other man snapped cuffs on his ankles and attached a steel chain to his ankle cuff and his wrist cuffs.

"This is all a mistake," said Rob, loudly. "I need to speak to a lawyer."

One guard patted him down, took his phone and wallet, and put them in a plastic bag, and sealed it.

260

Two men led him into an elevator without speaking any more than was necessary to get him to comply. One of them put a key into the elevator panel and pressed for the sixth floor.

The elevator rattled as it went up. The door opened and they were in a reception area with dark wood paneling. No one was working at the reception desk. They pushed him down a corridor to the left and into a room with bars on the windows and metal chairs and a table bolted to the floor. A Perspex sheet hung between one side of the table and the other. It extended beyond the table so that the room was almost separated into two parts.

They left him there without saying anything. One of them still held the plastic bag with his phone in it.

He looked out through the window bars over office buildings and in the distance saw a glimpse of a gray sea. How had it come to this? He'd given details of his vaccine to everyone, he'd cooperated with TOTALVACS, and all he wanted was to find out if the Russians had been lying. To find out if Jackie was still alive.

This was all wrong.

The door of the room opened. A tall woman with long blonde hair strode in. She was followed by a young man with a crew cut. They were both wearing black face masks. The woman stood by the table, on the other side to where he was.

"Please sit, Dr. McNeil," she said.

Rob sat.

The woman held an ID card up for him to read her name. Then she and the man held their cards up toward a security camera in the corner of the ceiling. The man passed her a thick brown folder. She opened it and placed it on the table. In it lay an inch-thick stack of printouts. His picture was stapled in a corner of the top sheet.

"How long have you been working for the Russian government?" asked the woman, as she placed a hand on the folder.

"I do not work for the Russian government," said Rob.

The woman turned over a few pages, looked up at him. "But you gave a lecture recently at a scientific institute in Moscow, is that correct?"

"I was obliged to do that in exchange for the help I'd received from a Russian government official," he said. He was doing his best to control his frustration. It wasn't easy.

"So, you were repaying a debt to the Russian government?"

Rob looked straight at her. "There was no payment for what I did, no money involved."

"Is a private jet flight from Beijing to Moscow a free service these days?"

"I was with two State Department staff. I arranged the flight to help them get out of China too."

The woman looked down at the page in front of her. "You met with Russian Embassy operatives here in Washington on multiple occasions over the past few days. Please explain what those meetings were about."

"I was told that my wife, Jackie, was still alive and that if I cooperated with the Russian Embassy that she would be returned to me."

"And you agreed to cooperate?" asked the woman.

"No, that's not the way it is! They threw me out because I wouldn't do what they wanted!"

The woman looked up. "Do not shout, Dr. McNeil. I have perfectly good hearing. We understand you agreed to cooperate with them and that when they asked you to go further, you then objected. Is that a fair assessment?"

Rob put his hands flat on the table. "No, I didn't . . . I did not cooperate. I would be with her now if I had." He pressed his fist to his mouth. It felt as if a hole had opened up under him.

"I refused to do what I was asked, yes. And now what I get is this?" He waved around him at the room and at the shackles on his hands and feet.

"What did the Russians want from you?"

He leaned forward. "They wanted me to say I've been trying to slow down the production of my vaccine on the prompting of someone who works with the Biden campaign."

"You did try to slow the production of a vaccine. That is correct, isn't it?"

He didn't reply.

The woman and the man looked at each other.

"Thank you, Dr. McNeil. This questioning session has now ended." She looked up at the camera pod in the corner of the room.

"End interview," she said.

73

"Are the Wang Hu interview recordings accessible?" asked Faith. She kept her phone to her ear, stood, walked to the window. The street outside was quiet. Because of the advice to work from home and the BLM protests, a lot of people were not coming into the center of DC anymore.

"Yep, video and audio are available to access as you need."

"Are you finished interviewing for today?"

"After a two-hour break, we're going to ask him to confirm a few details. We're putting together a task force with the FBI, Faith. You can request to be included, but your work at TOTALVACS is probably enough for you right now, yes?"

"Probably. I'll take a look at the video, thanks."

She logged onto the secure State Department interrogations videos drive using facial ID and a one-time password sent to the State app.

The recording showed Wang in a hospital bed and a female State Department employee introducing herself to him.

"Where's Faith?" asked Wang, looking up at the camera.

"I'll be your contact from now on," said the woman. She gave her name and asked Wang a few basic questions about his identity. Then she gave him a speech about the State Department witness protection program, which would allow him to live in his choice of location with a completely new identity, including a cash amount and rent-free apartment.

She made it sound like winning the lottery.

Wang didn't reply.

"Does the Chinese government deliberately spread the Coronavirus?" asked the woman.

Wang shook his head. "No, this is not official Chinese government policy. A secret group within China does this," said Wang.

"What group?" said the woman.

"I need to know I will be protected," he said. "Our deal has to be agreed properly before I will say more."

The recording went blank.

They were on the verge of a real breakthrough. She let her breath out, as the magnitude of what she'd seen sank in and a doubt with it. Was it too good to be true? Confirmation from another source would certainly help prove it. She closed her laptop. That was why her upcoming meeting was so crucial. If she could get Gong Dao to come over, they would have enough to go public. She paced the room.

She had three hours to go before her meeting with Gong Dao.

The Jefferson Hotel lay half a mile north of Lafayette Square, far enough away from any demonstrations to be safe, but near enough to still get a whiff of tear gas in the air if things got nasty again. The fact that Gong Dao had agreed to meet her there meant that the Chinese Embassy probably had a set of rooms permanently booked at the hotel, and that Gong Dao was high enough up the totem pole at the embassy that she could do whatever she wanted.

Gong Dao had presumably also been informed of Wang's probable defection. That meant her agreeing to the meeting had benefits for her too. She'd probably been sent to the meeting in the hope that she'd find out how much Wang had revealed already.

Faith called the officer in charge of overseeing her meet. The man was a long-time State Department, Chinese Embassy liaison staffer. He sounded relaxed as he took the call.

"Any reason we should be concerned for your safety, Ms. Gordon?" he asked.

"No, I expect this will be friendly. Just make sure the library where we are meeting has at least two cameras working and good audio. Good enough to record a pin drop," said Faith.

"Sure, we've got all that set up for you," said the officer. "Just get there on time and our extraction team will be in a room down the hall if anything gets nasty."

"It won't," said Faith.

She put a call in to the FBI special agent in charge of interrogating McNeil. He didn't answer. He probably knew the call was from her. Faith sighed, looked around. She'd have loved to moan to someone about the FBI going out on a limb, but she couldn't do that, no matter how she felt.

A complaint about McNeil had been made to their Washington office and they'd run with it. Who had complained, the evidence provided, and how they knew to pick him up outside the Russian Embassy were all interesting questions. But at least they had informed State, as a friendly gesture, when they'd seen a State Department flag on his record online, though it hadn't stopped them picking him up.

The evidence they'd been given must have been hot too, from someone they trusted. The FBI was full of agents looking to make a name for themselves and Rob had gone too far, if what she'd heard in the one call she did manage to have with the agent in charge was true.

Bishop had claimed, "We don't need him anymore," when Faith had told him about Rob's arrest.

"His partners have signed the agreement," Bishop had continued. "We may even get out of some of the payments if he's shown to be an agent of a foreign power. It will allow us to hold up payments and force them to sue us for them. Don't do anything to help him, Faith. He's getting what he deserves for believing the Ruskies."

What Faith kept thinking about, as she packed away her laptop and stored it in one of the lockers in TOTALVACS, was what the hell the Russians had been up to, leading McNeil on like that? Was it all really just them trying to get him to mess things up at TOTALVACS?

What was their game? If it was to destroy McNeil's career, they'd certainly achieved that.

She headed down to the car waiting in the underground car park for her.

74

Vladimir opened the door of the meeting room. A woman was standing at the window, looking out over the front gate to the embassy.

"When will I be free to go?" said the woman, in a British accent, as she turned to Vladimir.

"We have a few extra recordings we need you to make. Then you can go." Vladimir stood beside her.

"I would not have agreed to do this if I'd known where all this was going," she said.

"Be patient," said Vladimir. "Your reward is coming." He looked at his watch. "Everything will work out. Trust me."

75

Faith looked at the text message. *In the Quill Bar*, it read. They were heading up 16th Street. The Jefferson Hotel was up ahead on the left. She would be ten minutes late. He deserved it.

She messaged the officer in charge of her meet with Gong Dao. He'd replied with a thumbs up. It was going to be a busy afternoon.

A minute later, the Chevy pulled around and stopped in front of the hotel. Two red and gray taxis waited outside. A closed sign stood outside the hotel, but the taxis showed that it was still serving residents, most likely people who were staying there when the virus first passed through the city.

The French Beaux-Arts style to the hotel appealed to the monied Europeans who stayed there, but not to Faith. It was all a bit fake to her. She walked in under the iron and glass entry canopy into the white and pale-blue decorated reception hall with its black and white checkerboard marble floor. She walked straight across and into the Quill Bar.

Tension in her gut tugged at her. She knew this had to be done but was not looking forward to it.

She saw Senator Harmforth as soon as she entered the bar. He was nursing what looked like a double bourbon on the rocks. He stood as she approached and gave her a wide smile. He wasn't wearing a mask. She was.

"Sit down, honey," he said. "It sure is great to see you. I got a room upstairs too." He raised his eyebrows. "You sure you need that mask? I ain't got it."

Every part of her was wound up now, waiting for his reaction, looking forward so much to giving him what he amply deserved. "Senator, this is not what you think." She stopped, watched as his face slowly changed, as he took in the very different look on her face, her tone and what it most likely meant.

He blinked, twice. "What's up?" he said. He'd dropped the honey.

"It's over. We're over," she said. "I thought you deserved better than a text, but please, do not try to persuade me otherwise. It's over."

His face looked like a balloon being deflated.

"Hold on now," he said. "You can't just throw me away like that. I was planning to introduce you to my family this weekend."

She shook her head. Her heart pounded. She was looking forward to getting this over with. "You've been saying that for the last two months," she said. She spoke slowly now. "It's over, say goodbye nicely. That's all we've got to do now."

His expression had paled at first, but now his cheeks were getting red. The tension in the air was almost visible.

"Fuck you," he said, softly. "I was going to ditch you anyway. I don't need your skinny ass. Go to hell, Faith Gordon."

A waiter in a white shirt had stopped nearby, stared, and almost ran away, as he picked up the vibes.

Faith leaned toward the senator. "You should go back to Oregon. Don't say you weren't warned."

His mouth opened as he tried to take in the implications of what Faith had just said. He was struggling, trying to work out what she meant.

His mouth twitched.

A cold shiver ran down her back. Was this the moment he'd go crazy?

"Goodbye," she said. She stepped back. "No hard feelings?" She took another step back, her gaze still on him.

His mouth opened, then closed. "You bitch," he said, icily. "Have you been planning this all along? Have you been playing me with all your questions about the Chinese?"

Faith turned and walked toward the door.

"Bitch," she heard again from behind her. She had a strong urge to go back and either slap his ugly face or punch him.

But she had another appointment to go to. An important appointment. The reason she'd asked the senator to meet her here. She headed for the resident's library. Her phone buzzed as she walked. It was a message from the agent in charge.

Where are you?

On my way, she replied.

She looked at the auto audio-recording app on her phone and pressed on the last recording link. She held the phone to her ear. The app had recorded everything, perfectly.

She'd stepped over the line with the senator, but both of them had a lot to lose and the pay-off, the information about what the White House was planning, had helped her a lot. The career risk had been worth it. So far.

271

Laurence O'Bryan

None of this would matter, of course, if the next meeting went well. Every previous indiscretion she'd ever made would be forgotten.

She found the restrooms, adjusted her blouse, pushed a few stray hairs behind an ear. It was time.

76

New Jersey, June 6th, 2020

Washington Memorial Hospital in Camden, New Jersey, ninety miles from New York City, deals with both military and civilian patients. The facility had been designated a Coronavirus treatment center. It had been dealing with a steady flow of Coronavirus patients since March 2020.

The secure military section of the hospital provides high security patient beds for military prisoners, high-ranking officers, and other special cases requiring sophisticated medical care.

Wang Hu was in the high-security section at the back of the building. Access was by monitored door entry and a thorough staff screening system.

It was two-thirty in the afternoon. The senior State Department staffer in charge of the interrogation was finished for the day. Her plan was to question Wang for about ninety minutes each morning to allow time for his recovery.

The senior nurse in charge of the ward was on a break. Details of rosters were available on the secure online hospital staff rota system. Her assistant was with a patient. The two other nurses for the ward were constantly busy.

The Military Police officers at the locked door to the ward checked the nurse's pass before she pushed her hospital drugs trolley through the door.

"You're early," said the young black officer. He looked at her directly, comparing the picture on her laminated ID pass with her face.

The Asian-looking nurse smiled at him and bowed slightly.

The young man let her through. She went straight to Wang Hu's room, knocked on the door, waited a few seconds, and then pushed in. He was sleeping. A drip ran from his arm. She took the syringe lying in the steel tray on her trolley, opened the access port in the primary tubing, and emptied the contents of the syringe into the tubing, then closed the port again.

Not even a puncture wound would be visible.

As she pushed her trolley through the door, she looked back. His eyelids were moving. He was dreaming.

77

Washington DC, June 6th, 2020

Faith entered the library of the Jefferson Hotel and looked around. There was nobody in the room. She was a few minutes late. Had Gong Dao gone already? The room was lined with bookshelves filled with leather-bound books. Glass cases held special editions and Jefferson memorabilia.

Small mahogany tables and sets of deep-cushioned leather chairs allowed for intimate meetings or quiet reading. The only noise was a faint hum from the air conditioning.

Faith sat in a seat in the corner, with a view of the only door, and near the window overlooking the street outside and the branches of a tree filled with new leaves.

She checked her phone. No message from Gong Dao. Had she blown it?

It was sixteen minutes to three. She was very late.

The door of the room swung open. Gong Dao walked in, her head high. She had on a dark gray suit with a tight skirt that showed her curves. In her hand, she held her smartphone. On her face, she wore a gray face mask.

Faith wasn't wearing one. It wasn't required in the hotel or by the State Department, though some people wore them voluntarily.

Gong Dao looked around, then came toward Faith. She stopped about six feet away. She gave Faith a nod and then started talking fast in Mandarin.

"We finally meet," she said. "I hope you aren't disappointed that your senator friend has been playing the field." She didn't wait for Faith to reply but went on.

"Can we sit away from the window," she asked. She pointed at a table in the corner of the room. Faith moved to it.

As they sat, Gong Dao said. "I must tell you I have no expectations regarding the senator. None at all." She let out a small laugh, shrugged. "There are so many opportunities for women like us, no?" She waited a few seconds this time for Faith to reply, but when she didn't, she started talking again.

"You would do well working for our embassy as a part-time liaison person. Would you consider it?" She looked around, wide-eyed, as if looking for a camera. "Our embassy pays very well, and we don't ask for any secrets, just for you to tell us your views on our policies." She put her head to the side "It's very like being on a consumer research panel. Would that interest you?" She crossed her legs. "We so need bright people, you see. Too many old-timers. Did I tell you the pay is very good?"

"Yes," said Faith. "You told me, twice, but I'm more interested in why you fell out with your friend, a Mr. Wang Hu." Faith paused.

Gong Dao breathed in.

"Have you ever had a man obsessed with you?" she asked, leaning forward.

Faith made a "maybe" gesture with her hands going wide.

"I am sure you know it is a terrible thing. You have stalking laws here in the United States, but in China, the best thing to do, for the man's sake, is to give them no illusions."

"You know he's in hospital?" said Faith.

"Yes, yes, you are so kind to look after him after that terrible incident in the service area."

"Do you have any idea why someone from your embassy would try to kill him?"

Gong Dao shook her head. "He was an obsessive." She leaned toward Faith, dropped her voice. "I think he overstepped some personal relationship. That is all."

"It's nice to see you are so concerned about him," said Faith. Her phone buzzed. She looked at the text message. *Wang Hu found dead*, it read. Her eyebrow twitched. She pressed her lips together.

"Bad news?" asked Gong Dao.

Faith opened her mouth, closed it, looked at her phone, then at Gong Dao. The moment lengthened.

"I am sorry. Mr. Wang Hu has been found dead," she said. She stared at Gong Dao, looking for a reaction.

"So sad," said Gong Dao, her tone going high. But her expression did not change. She might have been talking about a distant relative being ill.

"Yes, it is. Please give our condolences to his family," said Faith.

Gong Dao looked at her as if she wanted to move the conversation on.

"You don't seem very surprised," said Faith.

"Do not use death, to bring death to life. That is what Confucius said." Gong Dao bowed.

"There's something else I want to talk to you about," said Faith.

277

Gong Dao looked at her nails. Her red nail polish was perfect.

"We have evidence that someone at your embassy has been making payments to a political campaign in Oregon. Such payments would be an illegal interference in the affairs of the United States." Faith tapped at her phone. She turned it to Gong Dao.

"You are the person who met with several individuals here in Washington, people who traveled from Oregon. These pictures show the meetings." She flicked through a few pictures, paused. Gong Dao peered down at the screen.

"My question is, were these meetings approved by your government?"

Gong Dao looked toward the door.

"Please don't try to leave. There are State Department agents outside the door."

"I have nothing more to say to you," said Gong Dao, icily. "You cannot stop me leaving." She stood up.

78

Washington DC, June 6th, 2020

Rob took a sip from the plastic bottle of water he'd been given for his lunch. He'd been allowed to go to the toilet, but when he came back to the interview room, he was shackled from a chain attached to the cuffs around his feet to a metal ring in the floor, and from his handcuffs to a metal ring on the table.

He'd been alone for what seemed like hours. Then the same two FBI interrogators came back into the room.

"When can I call a lawyer?" he asked.

The older FBI man said, "The head of a federal agency may request from the President a temporary exemption from the right to have an attorney present, when such an exemption is determined to be in the interest of national security."

"You're joking," said Rob.

"No, I am not. And it will be a lot easier for you, McNeil, if you admit to cooperating with the Russians and provide full disclosure at this time, to help us with our ongoing investigations into matters of national security."

The woman leaned toward him. "We will tell the judge that you cooperated. Your sentence will be greatly reduced if you do cooperate now."

"I did nothing wrong," said Rob, his voice rising.

She shook her head. "We have pictures of you talking with a Russian agent in a park near where you were staying here in DC, McNeil, and we have audio recordings of those meetings." She pointed at him. "We obtained a federal warrant for these recordings, so they will be admissible, and you can be clearly heard agreeing to help the Russians in the recordings. We will use these recordings in court."

Rob let out a frustrated groan. "I agreed to help them to try to get my wife released. I didn't do anything for them," said Rob. "I did nothing wrong."

The agent looked at her phone, scrolled down a page. "Did you request a delay in a vaccine production schedule?"

He groaned again. "That was a suggestion to improve the effectiveness of a vaccine I developed."

"Which would delay that vaccine," said the woman. "And which you submitted at the request of your Russian handler."

Rob didn't reply. The sinking feeling inside him had just gone a few miles deeper.

"This is an open and shut case, McNeil," said the male agent. "Why don't you come clean and cooperate?"

"I am. I was trying to get my wife released by the Russians," said Rob, slowly now, emphasizing each word. "Nothing I did produced any results for them."

The two agents looked at each other.

"It looks like you got what you expected from the Russians, McNeil. We saw someone claiming to be your wife on Fox News this morning. She was appealing for you to be released."

Rob's mouth opened. He could feel the blood draining from his face. She'd been released. He'd been right to string Vladimir along. But why had he decided to release Jackie now?

Or was this all another trick?

"Are you sure that person is my wife?"

"This is her, yes?" said the male agent, holding a large screen smartphone toward him.

Rob squinted, leaned to the phone. A still image from a TV news program filled the screen. A hole opened up inside him, sucking all hope in.

"That's not my wife," he said, angrily.

He stuck his chin out. The bastard had been tricking him all along. They'd probably tipped off the FBI too. And now he was in prison and couldn't help TOTALVACS. The Russians must think they'd won.

He pointed at the screen.

"You should arrest this woman and find out how the Russians tricked me," he said. He breathed in deeply. "I don't regret any of it," he said. "I had to take any chance to save her and I'd do it again."

The female agent shook her head, slowly. "That interview was provided to the TV station in a video file. We have no idea where this woman is. We already checked that out." She leaned forward. "You're lying now, aren't you? There's more to this."

Rob let out an indignant gasp. "What are you talking about?"

"What else have you been doing for the Russians?" said the man.

79

Faith pointed at Gong Dao's chair. "Sit back down and listen to what I have to say."

Gong Dao stayed on her feet.

"I am going to give you another option," said Faith.

Gong Dao's expression became a sneer. "I won't betray the motherland," she said.

"Did you know you're going straight to prison camp when you get back to Beijing?" said Faith. "Have you ever received an urgent summons to return?" She kept her expression hard, matching Gong Dao's.

Gong Dao shook her head, quickly. Her eyes blazed defiance.

"Well, you'll get one soon, after we tell them about the rogue operation you've been running without permission for a secret society. Your Chanel suits and handbags aren't going to be much use to you in a freezing forced labor camp."

"You don't scare me," said Gong Dao.

"They will disown you. We've seen it. You must have too. And they'll denounce you at your high-speed trial. I don't expect they'll even name the yellow dragons. That would acknowledge their existence. A simple corruption trial covers a lot of sins in China."

"That's ridiculous. My government will not believe you."

"They will if we send them some proof."

"You have no proof," Gong Dao scoffed.

"Sorry; your good friend Wang Hu explained how the both of you were working for the yellow dragon society. He said it will be easy to verify your meetings together and his meetings with the society in New York and Beijing."

"I'm not part of whatever he was up to."

"You want to risk it?"

"Yes," she said vehemently.

"We have more evidence too. Do you think your ambassador will support you after we show him Senator Harmforth's testimony against you?" It was a step further than what they had on Gong Dao now, but they could get it. Faith was sure of that.

"Harmforth has already claimed he was involved with you to get evidence against your mother country, to prove your role in spreading the virus. He did the right thing for America. He also claims you shared a lot of useful information with him."

Gong Dao's mouth was moving, as if she wanted to spit something out.

Her phone buzzed. She looked at the screen.

She bit her lip.

"You can have a new life, a new name, an apartment in any city, anywhere. You'll be free," said Faith.

Gong Dao turned her head. She had a puzzled look on her face.

A flash of light filled the room, forcing hot air into lungs and eyes and ears.

The force of the explosion ripped the Jefferson library room apart. Masonry, plaster, and wood turned into flying weapons in a split second.

The noise echoed for long seconds and then a rumbling started as joists settled and pale fragments of wall and floor fell for another a half minute.

The explosive compound identified later was Russian, but it could have been used by any number of actors.

The Chinese Embassy had a security team at the site within ten minutes. It was claimed that they were preparing for a security test nearby. It was likely they were tracking Gong Dao.

Jim Stein, who'd been the Central Intelligence Agency's liaison for Faith's meeting monitoring team, was the first US official to enter the library. He coughed from the thick clouds of plaster dust and could barely see. He'd raced into the room without even putting on a face mask.

He found Faith after Gong Dao, who was clearly dead, a piece of wood in her chest, her eyes wide, unmoving.

And Faith wasn't dead.

He carried her out of the library, stumbling on debris, but he didn't drop her. There were risks carrying a wounded person, but there were also the risks of falling debris and her breathing being compromised by the dust.

A hotel worker was screaming at the top of her voice in the corridor. The man didn't stop as Jim carried Faith past him to the reception area, where dust was drifting and outside into the CIA minivan he had arrived in twenty minutes before.

"George Washington Hospital, fast," he shouted at the driver.

Faith's head was in his lap. He put his lips to hers and forced air into her mouth. There was no response. She wasn't breathing.

His heart pounded. He remembered a tour he'd been on in Iraq, when one of his team had died in his arms. He wasn't going to let Faith go.

"You got any water?" he shouted at the driver.

A bottle was handed to him. He opened it, poured a lot of it across Faith's dust smeared face.

He slapped her cheek.

"Come on, come back, come back," he shouted. There was no response.

The driver swerved around a corner.

He moved Faith so she was more on her side. He had to make sure she could breathe. He slapped her back. Once, then a second time.

"You know what you're doing?" shouted the driver.

Faith coughed.

Jim held her hand tight.

"You're going to make it," he whispered. "Hang in there."

80

Jim Stein shrugged. "Anyone would have done the same," he said.

Dr. Bishop, the lead CIA officer inside TOTALVACS, shook his head.

"The doctors told me she'd probably have died if she'd been left to bleed out in that library."

Jim adjusted the angle on his laptop. The secure video conferencing system he was using had a tendency to darken your face if you didn't have good light in the room.

"We think the Chinese did it, right?" said Bishop.

"They claim we did it."

"Yeah, and we almost killed one of our own. That's just bull crap."

"They say we killed Wang Hu as well," said Jim. "They claim we've been trying to get their officials to defect."

"That's as good as an admission," said Bishop. "They had to make sure she wouldn't spill the beans about them deliberately spreading the virus."

"What's our story for the media?"

"A gas leak," said Bishop. "Very unfortunate."

"Gong Dao was going to defect, wasn't she?" said Jim.

286

"That fake message we sent to her phone would have pushed her over the edge."

"What about McNeil? How long is he going to get?" said Jim.

"If TOTALVACS appoints him a good trial lawyer, he should be out by Christmas," said Bishop.

"I know someone who can probably get him out before that," said Jim.

"What do we know about this yellow dragon society Faith spoke about during the meeting with Gong Dao?" asked Bishop.

"Not a lot. Wang Hu mentioned them in his initial debrief. Faith used the information. She was bluffing, hoping to get a reaction."

"We'll have to keep digging," said Bishop.

Jim smiled, briefly. "Remember what Confucius said."

"What's that?" said Bishop.

"It doesn't matter how slowly you go, so long as you do not stop."

Before You Go!

If you can be persuaded **to write a reader review on Amazon, I'd greatly appreciate it.**

There are three novels in this series:

The Conspiracy

The Conspiracy II

The Conspiracy III